DISCOVER • CONNECT • TAKE ACTION

TROOP LEADER planner

IF FOUND, PLEASE RETURN TO:

....

....

....

Paper Co. x Est. 2019

Most Wild Simplicity Paper Co. books are available at special quantity discounts for bulk purchase for sales promotions, fundraising, and educational needs. Special books or book excerpts also can be created to fit specific needs. For details, write: hello@wildsimplicitypaper.com

Printed in the United States

Book Design by Wild Simplicity Paper Co.
wildsimplicitypaper.com

LOVE YOUR TROOP LEADER PLANNER?

PLEASE LEAVE A REVIEW ON AMAZON!

TABLE OF CONTENTS

TROOP LEADER & VOLUNTEER CONTACT INFORMATION

NAME:

☐ BACKGROUND CHECK

TROOP LEADER PHONE: (......)................ EMAIL:...

NOTES:

NAME:

☐ BACKGROUND CHECK

TROOP LEADER PHONE: (......)................ EMAIL:...

NOTES:

NAME:

☐ BACKGROUND CHECK

VOLUNTEER TROOP MEMBER:.......................................'S ☐ PARENT/GUARDIAN ☐ GRANDPARENT ☐ SIBLING ☐ OTHER:...............................

TROOP ROLE(S): ☐ TREASURER ☐ COOKIE MANAGER ☐ FALL PRODUCT MANAGER ☐ CHAPERONE ☐ DRIVER ☐ GENERAL HELPER ☐ OTHER:....................................

PHONE: (......)................ EMAIL:.. SPECIAL SKILLS:..

NOTES:

NAME:

☐ BACKGROUND CHECK

VOLUNTEER TROOP MEMBER:.......................................'S ☐ PARENT/GUARDIAN ☐ GRANDPARENT ☐ SIBLING ☐ OTHER:...............................

TROOP ROLE(S): ☐ TREASURER ☐ COOKIE MANAGER ☐ FALL PRODUCT MANAGER ☐ CHAPERONE ☐ DRIVER ☐ GENERAL HELPER ☐ OTHER:....................................

PHONE: (......)................ EMAIL:.. SPECIAL SKILLS:..

NOTES:

NAME:

☐ BACKGROUND CHECK

VOLUNTEER TROOP MEMBER:.......................................'S ☐ PARENT/GUARDIAN ☐ GRANDPARENT ☐ SIBLING ☐ OTHER:...............................

TROOP ROLE(S): ☐ TREASURER ☐ COOKIE MANAGER ☐ FALL PRODUCT MANAGER ☐ CHAPERONE ☐ DRIVER ☐ GENERAL HELPER ☐ OTHER:....................................

PHONE: (......)................ EMAIL:.. SPECIAL SKILLS:..

NOTES:

"My mother had a saying: Kamala, you may be the first to do many things, but make sure you're not the last."
VICE PRESIDENT KAMALA HARRIS

NAME: ☐ BACKGROUND CHECK

VOLUNTEER TROOP MEMBER:..'S ☐ PARENT/GUARDIAN ☐ GRANDPARENT ☐ SIBLING ☐ OTHER:................................

TROOP ROLE(S): ☐ TREASURER ☐ COOKIE MANAGER ☐ FALL PRODUCT MANAGER ☐ CHAPERONE ☐ DRIVER ☐ GENERAL HELPER ☐ OTHER:......................................

PHONE: (.......)................. EMAIL:.. SPECIAL SKILLS:..

NOTES:

NAME: ☐ BACKGROUND CHECK

VOLUNTEER TROOP MEMBER:..'S ☐ PARENT/GUARDIAN ☐ GRANDPARENT ☐ SIBLING ☐ OTHER:................................

TROOP ROLE(S): ☐ TREASURER ☐ COOKIE MANAGER ☐ FALL PRODUCT MANAGER ☐ CHAPERONE ☐ DRIVER ☐ GENERAL HELPER ☐ OTHER:......................................

PHONE: (.......)................. EMAIL:.. SPECIAL SKILLS:..

NOTES:

NAME: ☐ BACKGROUND CHECK

VOLUNTEER TROOP MEMBER:..'S ☐ PARENT/GUARDIAN ☐ GRANDPARENT ☐ SIBLING ☐ OTHER:................................

TROOP ROLE(S): ☐ TREASURER ☐ COOKIE MANAGER ☐ FALL PRODUCT MANAGER ☐ CHAPERONE ☐ DRIVER ☐ GENERAL HELPER ☐ OTHER:......................................

PHONE: (.......)................. EMAIL:.. SPECIAL SKILLS:..

NOTES:

NAME: ☐ BACKGROUND CHECK

VOLUNTEER TROOP MEMBER:..'S ☐ PARENT/GUARDIAN ☐ GRANDPARENT ☐ SIBLING ☐ OTHER:................................

TROOP ROLE(S): ☐ TREASURER ☐ COOKIE MANAGER ☐ FALL PRODUCT MANAGER ☐ CHAPERONE ☐ DRIVER ☐ GENERAL HELPER ☐ OTHER:......................................

PHONE: (.......)................. EMAIL:.. SPECIAL SKILLS:..

NOTES:

NAME: ☐ BACKGROUND CHECK

VOLUNTEER TROOP MEMBER:..'S ☐ PARENT/GUARDIAN ☐ GRANDPARENT ☐ SIBLING ☐ OTHER:................................

TROOP ROLE(S): ☐ TREASURER ☐ COOKIE MANAGER ☐ FALL PRODUCT MANAGER ☐ CHAPERONE ☐ DRIVER ☐ GENERAL HELPER ☐ OTHER:......................................

PHONE: (.......)................. EMAIL:.. SPECIAL SKILLS:..

NOTES:

VOLUNTEER CONTACT INFORMATION (CONTINUED)

NAME: ☐ BACKGROUND CHECK

VOLUNTEER TROOP MEMBER:..'S ☐ PARENT/GUARDIAN ☐ GRANDPARENT ☐ SIBLING ☐ OTHER:..............................

TROOP ROLE(S): ☐ TREASURER ☐ COOKIE MANAGER ☐ FALL PRODUCT MANAGER ☐ CHAPERONE ☐ DRIVER ☐ GENERAL HELPER ☐ OTHER:..............................

PHONE: (.......)................. EMAIL:.. SPECIAL SKILLS:..

NOTES:

NAME: ☐ BACKGROUND CHECK

VOLUNTEER TROOP MEMBER:..'S ☐ PARENT/GUARDIAN ☐ GRANDPARENT ☐ SIBLING ☐ OTHER:..............................

TROOP ROLE(S): ☐ TREASURER ☐ COOKIE MANAGER ☐ FALL PRODUCT MANAGER ☐ CHAPERONE ☐ DRIVER ☐ GENERAL HELPER ☐ OTHER:..............................

PHONE: (.......)................. EMAIL:.. SPECIAL SKILLS:..

NOTES:

NAME: ☐ BACKGROUND CHECK

VOLUNTEER TROOP MEMBER:..'S ☐ PARENT/GUARDIAN ☐ GRANDPARENT ☐ SIBLING ☐ OTHER:..............................

TROOP ROLE(S): ☐ TREASURER ☐ COOKIE MANAGER ☐ FALL PRODUCT MANAGER ☐ CHAPERONE ☐ DRIVER ☐ GENERAL HELPER ☐ OTHER:..............................

PHONE: (.......)................. EMAIL:.. SPECIAL SKILLS:..

NOTES:

NAME: ☐ BACKGROUND CHECK

VOLUNTEER TROOP MEMBER:..'S ☐ PARENT/GUARDIAN ☐ GRANDPARENT ☐ SIBLING ☐ OTHER:..............................

TROOP ROLE(S): ☐ TREASURER ☐ COOKIE MANAGER ☐ FALL PRODUCT MANAGER ☐ CHAPERONE ☐ DRIVER ☐ GENERAL HELPER ☐ OTHER:..............................

PHONE: (.......)................. EMAIL:.. SPECIAL SKILLS:..

NOTES:

NAME: ☐ BACKGROUND CHECK

VOLUNTEER TROOP MEMBER:..'S ☐ PARENT/GUARDIAN ☐ GRANDPARENT ☐ SIBLING ☐ OTHER:..............................

TROOP ROLE(S): ☐ TREASURER ☐ COOKIE MANAGER ☐ FALL PRODUCT MANAGER ☐ CHAPERONE ☐ DRIVER ☐ GENERAL HELPER ☐ OTHER:..............................

PHONE: (.......)................. EMAIL:.. SPECIAL SKILLS:..

NOTES:

"The world will see you the way you see you and treat you the way you treat yourself."
BEYONCE

NAME: ☐ BACKGROUND CHECK

VOLUNTEER TROOP MEMBER:..'S ☐ PARENT/GUARDIAN ☐ GRANDPARENT ☐ SIBLING ☐ OTHER:................................

TROOP ROLE(S): ☐ TREASURER ☐ COOKIE MANAGER ☐ FALL PRODUCT MANAGER ☐ CHAPERONE ☐ DRIVER ☐ GENERAL HELPER ☐ OTHER:......................................

PHONE: (.......)................. EMAIL:... SPECIAL SKILLS:...

NOTES:

NAME: ☐ BACKGROUND CHECK

VOLUNTEER TROOP MEMBER:..'S ☐ PARENT/GUARDIAN ☐ GRANDPARENT ☐ SIBLING ☐ OTHER:................................

TROOP ROLE(S): ☐ TREASURER ☐ COOKIE MANAGER ☐ FALL PRODUCT MANAGER ☐ CHAPERONE ☐ DRIVER ☐ GENERAL HELPER ☐ OTHER:......................................

PHONE: (.......)................. EMAIL:... SPECIAL SKILLS:...

NOTES:

NAME: ☐ BACKGROUND CHECK

VOLUNTEER TROOP MEMBER:..'S ☐ PARENT/GUARDIAN ☐ GRANDPARENT ☐ SIBLING ☐ OTHER:................................

TROOP ROLE(S): ☐ TREASURER ☐ COOKIE MANAGER ☐ FALL PRODUCT MANAGER ☐ CHAPERONE ☐ DRIVER ☐ GENERAL HELPER ☐ OTHER:......................................

PHONE: (.......)................. EMAIL:... SPECIAL SKILLS:...

NOTES:

NAME: ☐ BACKGROUND CHECK

VOLUNTEER TROOP MEMBER:..'S ☐ PARENT/GUARDIAN ☐ GRANDPARENT ☐ SIBLING ☐ OTHER:................................

TROOP ROLE(S): ☐ TREASURER ☐ COOKIE MANAGER ☐ FALL PRODUCT MANAGER ☐ CHAPERONE ☐ DRIVER ☐ GENERAL HELPER ☐ OTHER:......................................

PHONE: (.......)................. EMAIL:... SPECIAL SKILLS:...

NOTES:

NAME: ☐ BACKGROUND CHECK

VOLUNTEER TROOP MEMBER:..'S ☐ PARENT/GUARDIAN ☐ GRANDPARENT ☐ SIBLING ☐ OTHER:................................

TROOP ROLE(S): ☐ TREASURER ☐ COOKIE MANAGER ☐ FALL PRODUCT MANAGER ☐ CHAPERONE ☐ DRIVER ☐ GENERAL HELPER ☐ OTHER:......................................

PHONE: (.......)................. EMAIL:... SPECIAL SKILLS:...

NOTES:

VOLUNTEER CONTACT INFORMATION (CONTINUED)

NAME: ☐ BACKGROUND CHECK

VOLUNTEER TROOP MEMBER:.......................................'S ☐ PARENT/GUARDIAN ☐ GRANDPARENT ☐ SIBLING ☐ OTHER:................................

TROOP ROLE(S): ☐ TREASURER ☐ COOKIE MANAGER ☐ FALL PRODUCT MANAGER ☐ CHAPERONE ☐ DRIVER ☐ GENERAL HELPER ☐ OTHER:....................................

PHONE: (.......)................. EMAIL:... SPECIAL SKILLS:..

NOTES:

NAME: ☐ BACKGROUND CHECK

VOLUNTEER TROOP MEMBER:.......................................'S ☐ PARENT/GUARDIAN ☐ GRANDPARENT ☐ SIBLING ☐ OTHER:................................

TROOP ROLE(S): ☐ TREASURER ☐ COOKIE MANAGER ☐ FALL PRODUCT MANAGER ☐ CHAPERONE ☐ DRIVER ☐ GENERAL HELPER ☐ OTHER:....................................

PHONE: (.......)................. EMAIL:... SPECIAL SKILLS:..

NOTES:

NAME: ☐ BACKGROUND CHECK

VOLUNTEER TROOP MEMBER:.......................................'S ☐ PARENT/GUARDIAN ☐ GRANDPARENT ☐ SIBLING ☐ OTHER:................................

TROOP ROLE(S): ☐ TREASURER ☐ COOKIE MANAGER ☐ FALL PRODUCT MANAGER ☐ CHAPERONE ☐ DRIVER ☐ GENERAL HELPER ☐ OTHER:....................................

PHONE: (.......)................. EMAIL:... SPECIAL SKILLS:..

NOTES:

NAME: ☐ BACKGROUND CHECK

VOLUNTEER TROOP MEMBER:.......................................'S ☐ PARENT/GUARDIAN ☐ GRANDPARENT ☐ SIBLING ☐ OTHER:................................

TROOP ROLE(S): ☐ TREASURER ☐ COOKIE MANAGER ☐ FALL PRODUCT MANAGER ☐ CHAPERONE ☐ DRIVER ☐ GENERAL HELPER ☐ OTHER:....................................

PHONE: (.......)................. EMAIL:... SPECIAL SKILLS:..

NOTES:

NAME: ☐ BACKGROUND CHECK

VOLUNTEER TROOP MEMBER:.......................................'S ☐ PARENT/GUARDIAN ☐ GRANDPARENT ☐ SIBLING ☐ OTHER:................................

TROOP ROLE(S): ☐ TREASURER ☐ COOKIE MANAGER ☐ FALL PRODUCT MANAGER ☐ CHAPERONE ☐ DRIVER ☐ GENERAL HELPER ☐ OTHER:....................................

PHONE: (.......)................. EMAIL:... SPECIAL SKILLS:..

NOTES:

SERVICE UNIT:

MEETING SCHEDULE: .... MEETING LOCATION: ....

POSITION:

NAME: ....

PHONE: (.......)..

EMAIL: ....

NOTES:

POSITION:

NAME: ....

PHONE: (.......)..

EMAIL: ....

NOTES:

POSITION:

NAME: ....

PHONE: (.......)..

EMAIL: ....

NOTES:

POSITION:

NAME: ....

PHONE: (.......)..

EMAIL: ....

NOTES:

POSITION:

NAME: ....

PHONE: (.......)..

EMAIL: ....

NOTES:

POSITION:

NAME: ....

PHONE: (.......)..

EMAIL: ....

NOTES:

POSITION:

NAME: ....

PHONE: (.......)..

EMAIL: ....

NOTES:

POSITION:

NAME: ....

PHONE: (.......)..

EMAIL: ....

NOTES:

COUNCIL:

PHONE: (.....)............................. FAX: (.....)............................ EMAIL(S): ....

SERVICE CENTER ADDRESS: .... SERVICE CENTER HOURS: ....

SHOP ADDRESS: .... SHOP HOURS: ....

WEBSITE: .... SOCIAL MEDIA: ....

NOTES:

POSITION:

NAME: ....

PHONE: (.......)..

EMAIL: ....

NOTES:

POSITION:

NAME: ....

PHONE: (.......)..

EMAIL: ....

NOTES:

POSITION:

NAME: ....

PHONE: (.......)..

EMAIL: ....

NOTES:

POSITION:

NAME: ....

PHONE: (.......)..

EMAIL: ....

NOTES:

POSITION:

NAME: ....

PHONE: (.......)..

EMAIL: ....

NOTES:

POSITION:

NAME: ....

PHONE: (.......)..

EMAIL: ....

NOTES:

TROOP ROSTER

NAME: BIRTHDAY: ....../....../...... AGE: ....

PHONE: (.......)................. EMAIL: .... SCHOOL: .... GRADE: ....

ADDRESS: .... LIVES WITH: ....

SHIRT SIZE: .... ALLERGIES: .... ON FILE: ☐ REGISTRATION ☐ HEALTH HISTORY ☐ PERMISSION SLIP ☐ OTHER: ....

PARENT/GUARDIAN: .... PHONE: (.......)................. EMAIL: ....

PARENT/GUARDIAN: .... PHONE: (.......)................. EMAIL: ....

NOTES:

☐ DAISY ☐ BROWNIE ☐ JUNIOR ☐ CADETTE ☐ SENIOR ☐ AMBASSADOR

NAME: BIRTHDAY: ....../....../...... AGE: ....

PHONE: (.......)................. EMAIL: .... SCHOOL: .... GRADE: ....

ADDRESS: .... LIVES WITH: ....

SHIRT SIZE: .... ALLERGIES: .... ON FILE: ☐ REGISTRATION ☐ HEALTH HISTORY ☐ PERMISSION SLIP ☐ OTHER: ....

PARENT/GUARDIAN: .... PHONE: (.......)................. EMAIL: ....

PARENT/GUARDIAN: .... PHONE: (.......)................. EMAIL: ....

NOTES:

☐ DAISY ☐ BROWNIE ☐ JUNIOR ☐ CADETTE ☐ SENIOR ☐ AMBASSADOR

NAME: BIRTHDAY: ....../....../...... AGE: ....

PHONE: (.......)................. EMAIL: .... SCHOOL: .... GRADE: ....

ADDRESS: .... LIVES WITH: ....

SHIRT SIZE: .... ALLERGIES: .... ON FILE: ☐ REGISTRATION ☐ HEALTH HISTORY ☐ PERMISSION SLIP ☐ OTHER: ....

PARENT/GUARDIAN: .... PHONE: (.......)................. EMAIL: ....

PARENT/GUARDIAN: .... PHONE: (.......)................. EMAIL: ....

NOTES:

☐ DAISY ☐ BROWNIE ☐ JUNIOR ☐ CADETTE ☐ SENIOR ☐ AMBASSADOR

TROOP ROSTER (CONTINUED)

NAME: BIRTHDAY: ...... / ...... / ...... AGE: ....

PHONE: (......)................ EMAIL: .... SCHOOL: .... GRADE: ....

ADDRESS: .... LIVES WITH: ....

SHIRT SIZE: .... ALLERGIES: .... ON FILE: ☐ REGISTRATION ☐ HEALTH HISTORY ☐ PERMISSION SLIP ☐ OTHER: ....

PARENT/GUARDIAN: .... PHONE: (......)................ EMAIL: ....

PARENT/GUARDIAN: .... PHONE: (......)................ EMAIL: ....

NOTES:

☐ DAISY ☐ BROWNIE ☐ JUNIOR ☐ CADETTE ☐ SENIOR ☐ AMBASSADOR

NAME: BIRTHDAY: ...... / ...... / ...... AGE: ....

PHONE: (......)................ EMAIL: .... SCHOOL: .... GRADE: ....

ADDRESS: .... LIVES WITH: ....

SHIRT SIZE: .... ALLERGIES: .... ON FILE: ☐ REGISTRATION ☐ HEALTH HISTORY ☐ PERMISSION SLIP ☐ OTHER: ....

PARENT/GUARDIAN: .... PHONE: (......)................ EMAIL: ....

PARENT/GUARDIAN: .... PHONE: (......)................ EMAIL: ....

NOTES:

☐ DAISY ☐ BROWNIE ☐ JUNIOR ☐ CADETTE ☐ SENIOR ☐ AMBASSADOR

NAME: BIRTHDAY: ...... / ...... / ...... AGE: ....

PHONE: (......)................ EMAIL: .... SCHOOL: .... GRADE: ....

ADDRESS: .... LIVES WITH: ....

SHIRT SIZE: .... ALLERGIES: .... ON FILE: ☐ REGISTRATION ☐ HEALTH HISTORY ☐ PERMISSION SLIP ☐ OTHER: ....

PARENT/GUARDIAN: .... PHONE: (......)................ EMAIL: ....

PARENT/GUARDIAN: .... PHONE: (......)................ EMAIL: ....

NOTES:

☐ DAISY ☐ BROWNIE ☐ JUNIOR ☐ CADETTE ☐ SENIOR ☐ AMBASSADOR

"So often in life, things that you regard as an impediment turn out to be great good fortune."

RUTH BADER GINSBURG

NAME:

BIRTHDAY: ...../...../..... AGE: ....

PHONE: (.......)................ EMAIL: .... SCHOOL: .... GRADE: ....

ADDRESS: .... LIVES WITH: ....

SHIRT SIZE: .... ALLERGIES: .... ON FILE: ☐ REGISTRATION ☐ HEALTH HISTORY ☐ PERMISSION SLIP ☐ OTHER: ....

PARENT/GUARDIAN: .... PHONE: (.......)................ EMAIL: ....

PARENT/GUARDIAN: .... PHONE: (.......)................ EMAIL: ....

NOTES:

☐ DAISY ☐ BROWNIE ☐ JUNIOR ☐ CADETTE ☐ SENIOR ☐ AMBASSADOR

NAME:

BIRTHDAY: ...../...../..... AGE: ....

PHONE: (.......)................ EMAIL: .... SCHOOL: .... GRADE: ....

ADDRESS: .... LIVES WITH: ....

SHIRT SIZE: .... ALLERGIES: .... ON FILE: ☐ REGISTRATION ☐ HEALTH HISTORY ☐ PERMISSION SLIP ☐ OTHER: ....

PARENT/GUARDIAN: .... PHONE: (.......)................ EMAIL: ....

PARENT/GUARDIAN: .... PHONE: (.......)................ EMAIL: ....

NOTES:

☐ DAISY ☐ BROWNIE ☐ JUNIOR ☐ CADETTE ☐ SENIOR ☐ AMBASSADOR

NAME:

BIRTHDAY: ...../...../..... AGE: ....

PHONE: (.......)................ EMAIL: .... SCHOOL: .... GRADE: ....

ADDRESS: .... LIVES WITH: ....

SHIRT SIZE: .... ALLERGIES: .... ON FILE: ☐ REGISTRATION ☐ HEALTH HISTORY ☐ PERMISSION SLIP ☐ OTHER: ....

PARENT/GUARDIAN: .... PHONE: (.......)................ EMAIL: ....

PARENT/GUARDIAN: .... PHONE: (.......)................ EMAIL: ....

NOTES:

☐ DAISY ☐ BROWNIE ☐ JUNIOR ☐ CADETTE ☐ SENIOR ☐ AMBASSADOR

TROOP ROSTER (CONTINUED)

NAME:
BIRTHDAY: ...../...../..... AGE: ....
PHONE: (.....)............ EMAIL: .... SCHOOL: .... GRADE: ....
ADDRESS: .... LIVES WITH: ....
SHIRT SIZE: .... ALLERGIES: .... ON FILE: ☐ REGISTRATION ☐ HEALTH HISTORY ☐ PERMISSION SLIP ☐ OTHER: ....
PARENT/GUARDIAN: .... PHONE: (.....)............ EMAIL: ....
PARENT/GUARDIAN: .... PHONE: (.....)............ EMAIL: ....
NOTES:

☐ DAISY ☐ BROWNIE ☐ JUNIOR ☐ CADETTE ☐ SENIOR ☐ AMBASSADOR

NAME:
BIRTHDAY: ...../...../..... AGE: ....
PHONE: (.....)............ EMAIL: .... SCHOOL: .... GRADE: ....
ADDRESS: .... LIVES WITH: ....
SHIRT SIZE: .... ALLERGIES: .... ON FILE: ☐ REGISTRATION ☐ HEALTH HISTORY ☐ PERMISSION SLIP ☐ OTHER: ....
PARENT/GUARDIAN: .... PHONE: (.....)............ EMAIL: ....
PARENT/GUARDIAN: .... PHONE: (.....)............ EMAIL: ....
NOTES:

☐ DAISY ☐ BROWNIE ☐ JUNIOR ☐ CADETTE ☐ SENIOR ☐ AMBASSADOR

NAME:
BIRTHDAY: ...../...../..... AGE: ....
PHONE: (.....)............ EMAIL: .... SCHOOL: .... GRADE: ....
ADDRESS: .... LIVES WITH: ....
SHIRT SIZE: .... ALLERGIES: .... ON FILE: ☐ REGISTRATION ☐ HEALTH HISTORY ☐ PERMISSION SLIP ☐ OTHER: ....
PARENT/GUARDIAN: .... PHONE: (.....)............ EMAIL: ....
PARENT/GUARDIAN: .... PHONE: (.....)............ EMAIL: ....
NOTES:

☐ DAISY ☐ BROWNIE ☐ JUNIOR ☐ CADETTE ☐ SENIOR ☐ AMBASSADOR

"We close the divide because we know to put our future first / We must first put our differences aside."

AWARD-WINNING POET AMANDA GORMAN

NAME:

BIRTHDAY: ...... / .... / .... AGE: ....

PHONE: (.......)................ EMAIL: .... SCHOOL: .... GRADE: ....

ADDRESS: .... LIVES WITH: ....

SHIRT SIZE: .... ALLERGIES: .... ON FILE: ☐ REGISTRATION ☐ HEALTH HISTORY ☐ PERMISSION SLIP ☐ OTHER: ....

PARENT/GUARDIAN: .... PHONE: (.......)................ EMAIL: ....

PARENT/GUARDIAN: .... PHONE: (.......)................ EMAIL: ....

NOTES:

☐ DAISY ☐ BROWNIE ☐ JUNIOR ☐ CADETTE ☐ SENIOR ☐ AMBASSADOR

NAME:

BIRTHDAY: ...... / .... / .... AGE: ....

PHONE: (.......)................ EMAIL: .... SCHOOL: .... GRADE: ....

ADDRESS: .... LIVES WITH: ....

SHIRT SIZE: .... ALLERGIES: .... ON FILE: ☐ REGISTRATION ☐ HEALTH HISTORY ☐ PERMISSION SLIP ☐ OTHER: ....

PARENT/GUARDIAN: .... PHONE: (.......)................ EMAIL: ....

PARENT/GUARDIAN: .... PHONE: (.......)................ EMAIL: ....

NOTES:

☐ DAISY ☐ BROWNIE ☐ JUNIOR ☐ CADETTE ☐ SENIOR ☐ AMBASSADOR

NAME:

BIRTHDAY: ...... / .... / .... AGE: ....

PHONE: (.......)................ EMAIL: .... SCHOOL: .... GRADE: ....

ADDRESS: .... LIVES WITH: ....

SHIRT SIZE: .... ALLERGIES: .... ON FILE: ☐ REGISTRATION ☐ HEALTH HISTORY ☐ PERMISSION SLIP ☐ OTHER: ....

PARENT/GUARDIAN: .... PHONE: (.......)................ EMAIL: ....

PARENT/GUARDIAN: .... PHONE: (.......)................ EMAIL: ....

NOTES:

☐ DAISY ☐ BROWNIE ☐ JUNIOR ☐ CADETTE ☐ SENIOR ☐ AMBASSADOR

TROOP ROSTER (CONTINUED)

NAME: BIRTHDAY: ...... / ...... / ...... AGE: ....

PHONE: (......) .... EMAIL: .... SCHOOL: .... GRADE: ....

ADDRESS: .... LIVES WITH: ....

SHIRT SIZE: .... ALLERGIES: .... ON FILE: ☐ REGISTRATION ☐ HEALTH HISTORY ☐ PERMISSION SLIP ☐ OTHER: ....

PARENT/GUARDIAN: .... PHONE: (......) .... EMAIL: ....

PARENT/GUARDIAN: .... PHONE: (......) .... EMAIL: ....

NOTES:

☐ DAISY ☐ BROWNIE ☐ JUNIOR ☐ CADETTE ☐ SENIOR ☐ AMBASSADOR

NAME: BIRTHDAY: ...... / ...... / ...... AGE: ....

PHONE: (......) .... EMAIL: .... SCHOOL: .... GRADE: ....

ADDRESS: .... LIVES WITH: ....

SHIRT SIZE: .... ALLERGIES: .... ON FILE: ☐ REGISTRATION ☐ HEALTH HISTORY ☐ PERMISSION SLIP ☐ OTHER: ....

PARENT/GUARDIAN: .... PHONE: (......) .... EMAIL: ....

PARENT/GUARDIAN: .... PHONE: (......) .... EMAIL: ....

NOTES:

☐ DAISY ☐ BROWNIE ☐ JUNIOR ☐ CADETTE ☐ SENIOR ☐ AMBASSADOR

NAME: BIRTHDAY: ...... / ...... / ...... AGE: ....

PHONE: (......) .... EMAIL: .... SCHOOL: .... GRADE: ....

ADDRESS: .... LIVES WITH: ....

SHIRT SIZE: .... ALLERGIES: .... ON FILE: ☐ REGISTRATION ☐ HEALTH HISTORY ☐ PERMISSION SLIP ☐ OTHER: ....

PARENT/GUARDIAN: .... PHONE: (......) .... EMAIL: ....

PARENT/GUARDIAN: .... PHONE: (......) .... EMAIL: ....

NOTES:

☐ DAISY ☐ BROWNIE ☐ JUNIOR ☐ CADETTE ☐ SENIOR ☐ AMBASSADOR

"You can never leave footprints that last if you are always walking on tiptoe."

LIBERIAN PEACE ACTIVIST LEYMAH GBOWEE

NAME: BIRTHDAY: ...../...../..... AGE: ....

PHONE: (.....)............ EMAIL: .... SCHOOL: .... GRADE: ....

ADDRESS: .... LIVES WITH: ....

SHIRT SIZE: .... ALLERGIES: .... ON FILE: ☐ REGISTRATION ☐ HEALTH HISTORY ☐ PERMISSION SLIP ☐ OTHER: ....

PARENT/GUARDIAN: .... PHONE: (.....)............ EMAIL: ....

PARENT/GUARDIAN: .... PHONE: (.....)............ EMAIL: ....

NOTES:

☐ DAISY ☐ BROWNIE ☐ JUNIOR ☐ CADETTE ☐ SENIOR ☐ AMBASSADOR

NAME: BIRTHDAY: ...../...../..... AGE: ....

PHONE: (.....)............ EMAIL: .... SCHOOL: .... GRADE: ....

ADDRESS: .... LIVES WITH: ....

SHIRT SIZE: .... ALLERGIES: .... ON FILE: ☐ REGISTRATION ☐ HEALTH HISTORY ☐ PERMISSION SLIP ☐ OTHER: ....

PARENT/GUARDIAN: .... PHONE: (.....)............ EMAIL: ....

PARENT/GUARDIAN: .... PHONE: (.....)............ EMAIL: ....

NOTES:

☐ DAISY ☐ BROWNIE ☐ JUNIOR ☐ CADETTE ☐ SENIOR ☐ AMBASSADOR

NAME: BIRTHDAY: ...../...../..... AGE: ....

PHONE: (.....)............ EMAIL: .... SCHOOL: .... GRADE: ....

ADDRESS: .... LIVES WITH: ....

SHIRT SIZE: .... ALLERGIES: .... ON FILE: ☐ REGISTRATION ☐ HEALTH HISTORY ☐ PERMISSION SLIP ☐ OTHER: ....

PARENT/GUARDIAN: .... PHONE: (.....)............ EMAIL: ....

PARENT/GUARDIAN: .... PHONE: (.....)............ EMAIL: ....

NOTES:

☐ DAISY ☐ BROWNIE ☐ JUNIOR ☐ CADETTE ☐ SENIOR ☐ AMBASSADOR

TROOP ROSTER (CONTINUED)

NAME:
BIRTHDAY: ....../......./....... AGE: ....

PHONE: (.......)................. EMAIL: .... SCHOOL: .... GRADE: ....

ADDRESS: .... LIVES WITH: ....

SHIRT SIZE: .... ALLERGIES: .... ON FILE: ☐ REGISTRATION ☐ HEALTH HISTORY ☐ PERMISSION SLIP ☐ OTHER: ....

PARENT/GUARDIAN: .... PHONE: (.......)................ EMAIL: ....

PARENT/GUARDIAN: .... PHONE: (.......)................ EMAIL: ....

NOTES:

☐ DAISY ☐ BROWNIE ☐ JUNIOR ☐ CADETTE ☐ SENIOR ☐ AMBASSADOR

NAME:
BIRTHDAY: ....../......./....... AGE: ....

PHONE: (.......)................. EMAIL: .... SCHOOL: .... GRADE: ....

ADDRESS: .... LIVES WITH: ....

SHIRT SIZE: .... ALLERGIES: .... ON FILE: ☐ REGISTRATION ☐ HEALTH HISTORY ☐ PERMISSION SLIP ☐ OTHER: ....

PARENT/GUARDIAN: .... PHONE: (.......)................ EMAIL: ....

PARENT/GUARDIAN: .... PHONE: (.......)................ EMAIL: ....

NOTES:

☐ DAISY ☐ BROWNIE ☐ JUNIOR ☐ CADETTE ☐ SENIOR ☐ AMBASSADOR

NAME:
BIRTHDAY: ....../......./....... AGE: ....

PHONE: (.......)................. EMAIL: .... SCHOOL: .... GRADE: ....

ADDRESS: .... LIVES WITH: ....

SHIRT SIZE: .... ALLERGIES: .... ON FILE: ☐ REGISTRATION ☐ HEALTH HISTORY ☐ PERMISSION SLIP ☐ OTHER: ....

PARENT/GUARDIAN: .... PHONE: (.......)................ EMAIL: ....

PARENT/GUARDIAN: .... PHONE: (.......)................ EMAIL: ....

NOTES:

☐ DAISY ☐ BROWNIE ☐ JUNIOR ☐ CADETTE ☐ SENIOR ☐ AMBASSADOR

"We will be known forever by the tracks we leave."
DAKOTA PROVERB

NAME:
BIRTHDAY: ...... / .... / .... AGE: ....
PHONE: (.......) .... EMAIL: .... SCHOOL: .... GRADE: ....
ADDRESS: .... LIVES WITH: ....
SHIRT SIZE: .... ALLERGIES: .... ON FILE: ☐ REGISTRATION ☐ HEALTH HISTORY ☐ PERMISSION SLIP ☐ OTHER: ....
PARENT/GUARDIAN: .... PHONE: (.......) .... EMAIL: ....
PARENT/GUARDIAN: .... PHONE: (.......) .... EMAIL: ....
NOTES:

☐ DAISY ☐ BROWNIE ☐ JUNIOR ☐ CADETTE ☐ SENIOR ☐ AMBASSADOR

NAME:
BIRTHDAY: ...... / .... / .... AGE: ....
PHONE: (.......) .... EMAIL: .... SCHOOL: .... GRADE: ....
ADDRESS: .... LIVES WITH: ....
SHIRT SIZE: .... ALLERGIES: .... ON FILE: ☐ REGISTRATION ☐ HEALTH HISTORY ☐ PERMISSION SLIP ☐ OTHER: ....
PARENT/GUARDIAN: .... PHONE: (.......) .... EMAIL: ....
PARENT/GUARDIAN: .... PHONE: (.......) .... EMAIL: ....
NOTES:

☐ DAISY ☐ BROWNIE ☐ JUNIOR ☐ CADETTE ☐ SENIOR ☐ AMBASSADOR

NAME:
BIRTHDAY: ...... / .... / .... AGE: ....
PHONE: (.......) .... EMAIL: .... SCHOOL: .... GRADE: ....
ADDRESS: .... LIVES WITH: ....
SHIRT SIZE: .... ALLERGIES: .... ON FILE: ☐ REGISTRATION ☐ HEALTH HISTORY ☐ PERMISSION SLIP ☐ OTHER: ....
PARENT/GUARDIAN: .... PHONE: (.......) .... EMAIL: ....
PARENT/GUARDIAN: .... PHONE: (.......) .... EMAIL: ....
NOTES:

☐ DAISY ☐ BROWNIE ☐ JUNIOR ☐ CADETTE ☐ SENIOR ☐ AMBASSADOR

TROOP ROSTER (CONTINUED)

NAME: BIRTHDAY: ...... / ...... / ...... AGE: ....

PHONE: (.......)................ EMAIL: .... SCHOOL: .... GRADE: ....

ADDRESS: .... LIVES WITH: ....

SHIRT SIZE: .... ALLERGIES: .... ON FILE: ☐ REGISTRATION ☐ HEALTH HISTORY ☐ PERMISSION SLIP ☐ OTHER: ....

PARENT/GUARDIAN: .... PHONE: (.......)................ EMAIL: ....

PARENT/GUARDIAN: .... PHONE: (.......)................ EMAIL: ....

NOTES:

☐ DAISY ☐ BROWNIE ☐ JUNIOR ☐ CADETTE ☐ SENIOR ☐ AMBASSADOR

NAME: BIRTHDAY: ...... / ...... / ...... AGE: ....

PHONE: (.......)................ EMAIL: .... SCHOOL: .... GRADE: ....

ADDRESS: .... LIVES WITH: ....

SHIRT SIZE: .... ALLERGIES: .... ON FILE: ☐ REGISTRATION ☐ HEALTH HISTORY ☐ PERMISSION SLIP ☐ OTHER: ....

PARENT/GUARDIAN: .... PHONE: (.......)................ EMAIL: ....

PARENT/GUARDIAN: .... PHONE: (.......)................ EMAIL: ....

NOTES:

☐ DAISY ☐ BROWNIE ☐ JUNIOR ☐ CADETTE ☐ SENIOR ☐ AMBASSADOR

NAME: BIRTHDAY: ...... / ...... / ...... AGE: ....

PHONE: (.......)................ EMAIL: .... SCHOOL: .... GRADE: ....

ADDRESS: .... LIVES WITH: ....

SHIRT SIZE: .... ALLERGIES: .... ON FILE: ☐ REGISTRATION ☐ HEALTH HISTORY ☐ PERMISSION SLIP ☐ OTHER: ....

PARENT/GUARDIAN: .... PHONE: (.......)................ EMAIL: ....

PARENT/GUARDIAN: .... PHONE: (.......)................ EMAIL: ....

NOTES:

☐ DAISY ☐ BROWNIE ☐ JUNIOR ☐ CADETTE ☐ SENIOR ☐ AMBASSADOR

TROOP BIRTHDAYS

AUGUST 2021	SEPTEMBER 2021	OCTOBER 2021

NOVEMBER 2021	DECEMBER 2021	JANUARY 2022

FEBRUARY 2022	MARCH 2022	APRIL 2022

MAY 2022	JUNE 2022	JULY 2022

YEAR AT-A-GLANCE

AUGUST 2021

S	M	T	W	T	F	S
1	2	3	4	5	6	7
8	9	10	11	12	13	14
15	16	17	18	19	20	21
22	23	24	25	26	27	28
29	30	31				

SEPTEMBER 2021

S	M	T	W	T	F	S
			1	2	3	4
5	6	7	8	9	10	11
12	13	14	15	16	17	18
19	20	21	22	23	24	25
26	27	28	29	30		

OCTOBER 2021

S	M	T	W	T	F	S
					1	2
3	4	5	6	7	8	9
10	11	12	13	14	15	16
17	18	19	20	21	22	23
24	25	26	27	28	29	30
31						

31: FOUNDER'S DAY

FEBRUARY 2022

S	M	T	W	T	F	S
		1	2	3	4	5
6	7	8	9	10	11	12
13	14	15	16	17	18	19
20	21	22	23	24	25	26
27	28					

22: WORLD THINKING DAY

MARCH 2022

S	M	T	W	T	F	S
		1	2	3	4	5
6	7	8	9	10	11	12
13	14	15	16	17	18	19
20	21	22	23	24	25	26
27	28	29	30	31		

12: GIRL SCOUTS' BIRTHDAY

APRIL 2022

S	M	T	W	T	F	S
					1	2
3	4	5	6	7	8	9
10	11	12	13	14	15	16
17	18	19	20	21	22	23
24	25	26	27	28	29	30

22: GIRL SCOUT LEADER'S DAY

"The work of today is the history of tomorrow and we are its makers."
JULIETTE GORDON LOW

NOVEMBER 2021

S	M	T	W	T	F	S
	1	2	3	4	5	6
7	8	9	10	11	12	13
14	15	16	17	18	19	20
21	22	23	24	25	26	27
28	29	30				

DECEMBER 2021

S	M	T	W	T	F	S
			1	2	3	4
5	6	7	8	9	10	11
12	13	14	15	16	17	18
19	20	21	22	23	24	25
26	27	28	29	30	31	

JANUARY 2022

S	M	T	W	T	F	S
						1
2	3	4	5	6	7	8
9	10	11	12	13	14	15
16	17	18	19	20	21	22
23	24	25	26	27	28	29
30	31					

MAY 2022

S	M	T	W	T	F	S
1	2	3	4	5	6	7
8	9	10	11	12	13	14
15	16	17	18	19	20	21
22	23	24	25	26	27	28
29	30	31				

JUNE 2022

S	M	T	W	T	F	S
			1	2	3	4
5	6	7	8	9	10	11
12	13	14	15	16	17	18
19	20	21	22	23	24	25
26	27	28	29	30		

JULY 2022

S	M	T	W	T	F	S
					1	2
3	4	5	6	7	8	9
10	11	12	13	14	15	16
17	18	19	20	21	22	23
24	25	26	27	28	29	30
31						

SUNDAY
MONDAY
TUESDAY
WEDNESDAY
THURSDAY
FRIDAY
SATURDAY

NOTES:

SUNDAY	MONDAY	TUESDAY	WEDNESDAY	THURSDAY	FRIDAY	SATURDAY

OTES:

....

SUNDAY	MONDAY	TUESDAY	WEDNESDAY	THURSDAY	FRIDAY	SATURDAY

NOTES:

SUNDAY	MONDAY	TUESDAY	WEDNESDAY	THURSDAY	FRIDAY	SATURDAY

OTES:

SUNDAY	MONDAY	TUESDAY	WEDNESDAY	THURSDAY	FRIDAY	SATURDAY

NOTES:

SUNDAY	MONDAY	TUESDAY	WEDNESDAY	THURSDAY	FRIDAY	SATURDAY

OTES:

SUNDAY	MONDAY	TUESDAY	WEDNESDAY	THURSDAY	FRIDAY	SATURDAY

NOTES:

SUNDAY	MONDAY	TUESDAY	WEDNESDAY	THURSDAY	FRIDAY	SATURDAY

TES :

SUNDAY	MONDAY	TUESDAY	WEDNESDAY	THURSDAY	FRIDAY	SATURDAY

NOTES:

SUNDAY	MONDAY	TUESDAY	WEDNESDAY	THURSDAY	FRIDAY	SATURDAY

OTES :

SUNDAY	MONDAY	TUESDAY	WEDNESDAY	THURSDAY	FRIDAY	SATURDAY

NOTES:

SUNDAY	MONDAY	TUESDAY	WEDNESDAY	THURSDAY	FRIDAY	SATURDAY

OTES:

MEETING PLANNER

DATE:

MEETING DETAILS

TIME: .... LOCATION: .... BADGE/JOURNEY/AWARD: ....

MEETING GOAL/THEME: ....

PRE-MEETING PREP:

SUPPLIES:

- ☐
- ☐
- ☐
- ☐
- ☐

VOLUNTEERS:

- ☐
- ☐
- ☐
- ☐
- ☐

REMINDERS:

MEETING STRUCTURE:

START-UP ACTIVITY:

OPENING:

BUSINESS:

ACTIVITIES:

(1)

(2)

(3)

(4)

(5)

CLEAN-UP & CLOSING:

NEXT MEETING:

REFLECTION:

DURING THIS MEETING, THE GIRLS...

☐ DISCOVERED ☐ CONNECTED ☐ TOOK ACTION

OUR ACTIVITIES WERE...

☐ GIRL-LED ☐ HANDS-ON ☐ COOPERATIVE

ATTENDANCE:

LOW ○ ○ ○ ○ ○ HIGH

ENJOYMENT:

LOW ○ ○ ○ ○ ○ HIGH

ENGAGEMENT:

LOW ○ ○ ○ ○ ○ HIGH

WHAT WAS MOST SUCCESSFUL?

WHAT COULD IMPROVE?

MEETING PLANNER

DATE:

MEETING DETAILS

TIME: .... LOCATION: .... BADGE/JOURNEY/AWARD: ....

MEETING GOAL/THEME: ....

PRE-MEETING PREP:

SUPPLIES:

- ☐
- ☐
- ☐
- ☐
- ☐

VOLUNTEERS:

- ☐
- ☐
- ☐
- ☐
- ☐

REMINDERS:

MEETING STRUCTURE:

START-UP ACTIVITY:

OPENING:

BUSINESS:

ACTIVITIES:

(1)

(2)

(3)

(4)

(5)

CLEAN-UP & CLOSING:

NEXT MEETING:

REFLECTION:

DURING THIS MEETING, THE GIRLS...

☐ DISCOVERED ☐ CONNECTED ☐ TOOK ACTION

OUR ACTIVITIES WERE...

☐ GIRL-LED ☐ HANDS-ON ☐ COOPERATIVE

ATTENDANCE:

LOW ○ ○ ○ ○ ○ HIGH

ENJOYMENT:

LOW ○ ○ ○ ○ ○ HIGH

ENGAGEMENT:

LOW ○ ○ ○ ○ ○ HIGH

WHAT WAS MOST SUCCESSFUL?

WHAT COULD IMPROVE?

MEETING PLANNER

DATE:

MEETING DETAILS

TIME: .... LOCATION: .... BADGE/JOURNEY/AWARD: ....

MEETING GOAL/THEME: ....

PRE-MEETING PREP:

SUPPLIES:

- ☐
- ☐
- ☐
- ☐
- ☐

VOLUNTEERS:

- ☐
- ☐
- ☐
- ☐
- ☐

REMINDERS:

MEETING STRUCTURE:

START-UP ACTIVITY:

OPENING:

BUSINESS:

ACTIVITIES:

(1)

(2)

(3)

(4)

(5)

CLEAN-UP & CLOSING:

NEXT MEETING:

REFLECTION:

DURING THIS MEETING, THE GIRLS...

☐ DISCOVERED ☐ CONNECTED ☐ TOOK ACTION

OUR ACTIVITIES WERE...

☐ GIRL-LED ☐ HANDS-ON ☐ COOPERATIVE

ATTENDANCE:

LOW ○ ○ ○ ○ ○ HIGH

ENJOYMENT:

LOW ○ ○ ○ ○ ○ HIGH

ENGAGEMENT:

LOW ○ ○ ○ ○ ○ HIGH

WHAT WAS MOST SUCCESSFUL?

WHAT COULD IMPROVE?

MEETING PLANNER

DATE:

MEETING DETAILS

TIME: .... LOCATION: .... BADGE/JOURNEY/AWARD: ....

MEETING GOAL/THEME: ....

PRE-MEETING PREP:

SUPPLIES:

- ☐
- ☐
- ☐
- ☐
- ☐

VOLUNTEERS:

- ☐
- ☐
- ☐
- ☐
- ☐

REMINDERS:

MEETING STRUCTURE:

START-UP ACTIVITY:

OPENING:

BUSINESS:

ACTIVITIES:

(1)

(2)

(3)

(4)

(5)

CLEAN-UP & CLOSING:

NEXT MEETING:

REFLECTION:

DURING THIS MEETING, THE GIRLS...

☐ DISCOVERED ☐ CONNECTED ☐ TOOK ACTION

OUR ACTIVITIES WERE...

☐ GIRL-LED ☐ HANDS-ON ☐ COOPERATIVE

ATTENDANCE:

LOW ○ ○ ○ ○ ○ HIGH

ENJOYMENT:

LOW ○ ○ ○ ○ ○ HIGH

ENGAGEMENT:

LOW ○ ○ ○ ○ ○ HIGH

WHAT WAS MOST SUCCESSFUL?

WHAT COULD IMPROVE?

MEETING PLANNER

DATE:

MEETING DETAILS

TIME: .... LOCATION: .... BADGE/JOURNEY/AWARD: ....

MEETING GOAL/THEME: ....

PRE-MEETING PREP:

SUPPLIES:

- ☐
- ☐
- ☐
- ☐
- ☐

VOLUNTEERS:

- ☐
- ☐
- ☐
- ☐
- ☐

REMINDERS:

MEETING STRUCTURE:

START-UP ACTIVITY:

OPENING:

BUSINESS:

ACTIVITIES:

(1)

(2)

(3)

(4)

(5)

CLEAN-UP & CLOSING:

NEXT MEETING:

REFLECTION:

DURING THIS MEETING, THE GIRLS...

☐ DISCOVERED ☐ CONNECTED ☐ TOOK ACTION

OUR ACTIVITIES WERE...

☐ GIRL-LED ☐ HANDS-ON ☐ COOPERATIVE

ATTENDANCE:

LOW ○ ○ ○ ○ ○ HIGH

ENJOYMENT:

LOW ○ ○ ○ ○ ○ HIGH

ENGAGEMENT:

LOW ○ ○ ○ ○ ○ HIGH

WHAT WAS MOST SUCCESSFUL?

WHAT COULD IMPROVE?

MEETING PLANNER

DATE:

MEETING DETAILS

TIME: .... LOCATION: .... BADGE/JOURNEY/AWARD: ....

MEETING GOAL/THEME: ....

PRE-MEETING PREP:

SUPPLIES:

- ☐
- ☐
- ☐
- ☐
- ☐

VOLUNTEERS:

- ☐
- ☐
- ☐
- ☐
- ☐

REMINDERS:

MEETING STRUCTURE:

START-UP ACTIVITY:

OPENING:

BUSINESS:

ACTIVITIES:

(1)

(2)

(3)

(4)

(5)

CLEAN-UP & CLOSING:

NEXT MEETING:

REFLECTION:

DURING THIS MEETING, THE GIRLS...

☐ DISCOVERED ☐ CONNECTED ☐ TOOK ACTION

OUR ACTIVITIES WERE...

☐ GIRL-LED ☐ HANDS-ON ☐ COOPERATIVE

ATTENDANCE:

LOW ○ ○ ○ ○ ○ HIGH

ENJOYMENT:

LOW ○ ○ ○ ○ ○ HIGH

ENGAGEMENT:

LOW ○ ○ ○ ○ ○ HIGH

WHAT WAS MOST SUCCESSFUL?

WHAT COULD IMPROVE?

MEETING PLANNER

DATE:

MEETING DETAILS

TIME: .... LOCATION: .... BADGE/JOURNEY/AWARD: ....

MEETING GOAL/THEME: ....

PRE-MEETING PREP:

SUPPLIES:

- ☐
- ☐
- ☐
- ☐
- ☐

VOLUNTEERS:

- ☐
- ☐
- ☐
- ☐
- ☐

REMINDERS:

MEETING STRUCTURE:

START-UP ACTIVITY:

OPENING:

BUSINESS:

ACTIVITIES:

(1)

(2)

(3)

(4)

(5)

CLEAN-UP & CLOSING:

NEXT MEETING:

REFLECTION:

DURING THIS MEETING, THE GIRLS...

☐ DISCOVERED ☐ CONNECTED ☐ TOOK ACTION

OUR ACTIVITIES WERE...

☐ GIRL-LED ☐ HANDS-ON ☐ COOPERATIVE

ATTENDANCE:

LOW ○ ○ ○ ○ ○ HIGH

ENJOYMENT:

LOW ○ ○ ○ ○ ○ HIGH

ENGAGEMENT:

LOW ○ ○ ○ ○ ○ HIGH

WHAT WAS MOST SUCCESSFUL?

WHAT COULD IMPROVE?

MEETING PLANNER

DATE:

MEETING DETAILS

TIME: .... LOCATION: .... BADGE/JOURNEY/AWARD: ....

MEETING GOAL/THEME: ....

PRE-MEETING PREP:

SUPPLIES:

- ☐
- ☐
- ☐
- ☐
- ☐

VOLUNTEERS:

- ☐
- ☐
- ☐
- ☐
- ☐

REMINDERS:

MEETING STRUCTURE:

START-UP ACTIVITY:

OPENING:

BUSINESS:

ACTIVITIES:

(1)

(2)

(3)

(4)

(5)

CLEAN-UP & CLOSING:

NEXT MEETING:

REFLECTION:

DURING THIS MEETING, THE GIRLS...

☐ DISCOVERED ☐ CONNECTED ☐ TOOK ACTION

OUR ACTIVITIES WERE...

☐ GIRL-LED ☐ HANDS-ON ☐ COOPERATIVE

ATTENDANCE:

LOW ○ ○ ○ ○ ○ HIGH

ENJOYMENT:

LOW ○ ○ ○ ○ ○ HIGH

ENGAGEMENT:

LOW ○ ○ ○ ○ ○ HIGH

WHAT WAS MOST SUCCESSFUL?

WHAT COULD IMPROVE?

MEETING PLANNER

DATE:

MEETING DETAILS

TIME: .... LOCATION: .... BADGE/JOURNEY/AWARD: ....

MEETING GOAL/THEME: ....

PRE-MEETING PREP:

SUPPLIES:

- ☐
- ☐
- ☐
- ☐
- ☐

VOLUNTEERS:

- ☐
- ☐
- ☐
- ☐
- ☐

REMINDERS:

MEETING STRUCTURE:

START-UP ACTIVITY:

OPENING:

BUSINESS:

ACTIVITIES:

(1)

(2)

(3)

(4)

(5)

CLEAN-UP & CLOSING:

NEXT MEETING:

REFLECTION:

DURING THIS MEETING, THE GIRLS...

☐ DISCOVERED ☐ CONNECTED ☐ TOOK ACTION

OUR ACTIVITIES WERE...

☐ GIRL-LED ☐ HANDS-ON ☐ COOPERATIVE

ATTENDANCE:

LOW ○ ○ ○ ○ ○ HIGH

ENJOYMENT:

LOW ○ ○ ○ ○ ○ HIGH

ENGAGEMENT:

LOW ○ ○ ○ ○ ○ HIGH

WHAT WAS MOST SUCCESSFUL?

WHAT COULD IMPROVE?

MEETING PLANNER

DATE:

MEETING DETAILS

TIME: .... LOCATION: .... BADGE/JOURNEY/AWARD: ....

MEETING GOAL/THEME: ....

PRE-MEETING PREP:

SUPPLIES:
- ☐
- ☐
- ☐
- ☐
- ☐

VOLUNTEERS:
- ☐
- ☐
- ☐
- ☐
- ☐

REMINDERS:

MEETING STRUCTURE:

START-UP ACTIVITY:

OPENING:

BUSINESS:

ACTIVITIES:

(1)

(2)

(3)

(4)

(5)

CLEAN-UP & CLOSING:

NEXT MEETING:

REFLECTION:

DURING THIS MEETING, THE GIRLS...

☐ DISCOVERED ☐ CONNECTED ☐ TOOK ACTION

OUR ACTIVITIES WERE...

☐ GIRL-LED ☐ HANDS-ON ☐ COOPERATIVE

ATTENDANCE:

LOW ○ ○ ○ ○ ○ HIGH

ENJOYMENT:

LOW ○ ○ ○ ○ ○ HIGH

ENGAGEMENT:

LOW ○ ○ ○ ○ ○ HIGH

WHAT WAS MOST SUCCESSFUL?

WHAT COULD IMPROVE?

MEETING PLANNER

DATE:

MEETING DETAILS

TIME: .... LOCATION: .... BADGE/JOURNEY/AWARD: ....

MEETING GOAL/THEME: ....

PRE-MEETING PREP:

SUPPLIES:

☐
☐
☐
☐
☐

VOLUNTEERS:

☐
☐
☐
☐
☐

REMINDERS:

MEETING STRUCTURE:

START-UP ACTIVITY:

OPENING:

BUSINESS:

ACTIVITIES:

(1)

(2)

(3)

(4)

(5)

CLEAN-UP & CLOSING:

NEXT MEETING:

REFLECTION:

DURING THIS MEETING, THE GIRLS...

☐ DISCOVERED ☐ CONNECTED ☐ TOOK ACTION

OUR ACTIVITIES WERE...

☐ GIRL-LED ☐ HANDS-ON ☐ COOPERATIVE

ATTENDANCE:

LOW ○ ○ ○ ○ ○ HIGH

ENJOYMENT:

LOW ○ ○ ○ ○ ○ HIGH

ENGAGEMENT:

LOW ○ ○ ○ ○ ○ HIGH

WHAT WAS MOST SUCCESSFUL?

WHAT COULD IMPROVE?

MEETING PLANNER

DATE:

MEETING DETAILS

TIME: .... LOCATION: .... BADGE/JOURNEY/AWARD: ....

MEETING GOAL/THEME: ....

PRE-MEETING PREP:

SUPPLIES:

- ☐
- ☐
- ☐
- ☐
- ☐

VOLUNTEERS:

- ☐
- ☐
- ☐
- ☐
- ☐

REMINDERS:

MEETING STRUCTURE:

START-UP ACTIVITY:

OPENING:

BUSINESS:

ACTIVITIES:

(1)

(2)

(3)

(4)

(5)

CLEAN-UP & CLOSING:

NEXT MEETING:

REFLECTION:

DURING THIS MEETING, THE GIRLS...

☐ DISCOVERED ☐ CONNECTED ☐ TOOK ACTION

OUR ACTIVITIES WERE...

☐ GIRL-LED ☐ HANDS-ON ☐ COOPERATIVE

ATTENDANCE:

LOW ○ ○ ○ ○ ○ HIGH

ENJOYMENT:

LOW ○ ○ ○ ○ ○ HIGH

ENGAGEMENT:

LOW ○ ○ ○ ○ ○ HIGH

WHAT WAS MOST SUCCESSFUL?

WHAT COULD IMPROVE?

MEETING PLANNER

DATE:

MEETING DETAILS

TIME: .... LOCATION: .... BADGE/JOURNEY/AWARD: ....

MEETING GOAL/THEME: ....

PRE-MEETING PREP:

SUPPLIES:

- ☐
- ☐
- ☐
- ☐
- ☐

VOLUNTEERS:

- ☐
- ☐
- ☐
- ☐
- ☐

REMINDERS:

MEETING STRUCTURE:

START-UP ACTIVITY:

OPENING:

BUSINESS:

ACTIVITIES:

(1)

(2)

(3)

(4)

(5)

CLEAN-UP & CLOSING:

NEXT MEETING:

REFLECTION:

DURING THIS MEETING, THE GIRLS...

☐ DISCOVERED ☐ CONNECTED ☐ TOOK ACTION

OUR ACTIVITIES WERE...

☐ GIRL-LED ☐ HANDS-ON ☐ COOPERATIVE

ATTENDANCE:

LOW ○ ○ ○ ○ ○ HIGH

ENJOYMENT:

LOW ○ ○ ○ ○ ○ HIGH

ENGAGEMENT:

LOW ○ ○ ○ ○ ○ HIGH

WHAT WAS MOST SUCCESSFUL?

WHAT COULD IMPROVE?

MEETING PLANNER

DATE:

MEETING DETAILS

TIME: .... LOCATION: .... BADGE/JOURNEY/AWARD: ....

MEETING GOAL/THEME: ....

PRE-MEETING PREP:

SUPPLIES:

- ☐
- ☐
- ☐
- ☐
- ☐

VOLUNTEERS:

- ☐
- ☐
- ☐
- ☐
- ☐

REMINDERS:

MEETING STRUCTURE:

START-UP ACTIVITY:

OPENING:

BUSINESS:

ACTIVITIES:

(1)

(2)

(3)

(4)

(5)

CLEAN-UP & CLOSING:

NEXT MEETING:

REFLECTION:

DURING THIS MEETING, THE GIRLS...

☐ DISCOVERED ☐ CONNECTED ☐ TOOK ACTION

OUR ACTIVITIES WERE...

☐ GIRL-LED ☐ HANDS-ON ☐ COOPERATIVE

ATTENDANCE:

LOW ○ ○ ○ ○ ○ HIGH

ENJOYMENT:

LOW ○ ○ ○ ○ ○ HIGH

ENGAGEMENT:

LOW ○ ○ ○ ○ ○ HIGH

WHAT WAS MOST SUCCESSFUL?

WHAT COULD IMPROVE?

MEETING PLANNER

DATE:

MEETING DETAILS

TIME: .... LOCATION: .... BADGE/JOURNEY/AWARD: ....

MEETING GOAL/THEME: ....

PRE-MEETING PREP:

SUPPLIES:
- ☐
- ☐
- ☐
- ☐
- ☐

VOLUNTEERS:
- ☐
- ☐
- ☐
- ☐
- ☐

REMINDERS:

MEETING STRUCTURE:

START-UP ACTIVITY:

OPENING:

BUSINESS:

ACTIVITIES:

(1)

(2)

(3)

(4)

(5)

CLEAN-UP & CLOSING:

NEXT MEETING:

REFLECTION:

DURING THIS MEETING, THE GIRLS...

☐ DISCOVERED ☐ CONNECTED ☐ TOOK ACTION

OUR ACTIVITIES WERE...

☐ GIRL-LED ☐ HANDS-ON ☐ COOPERATIVE

ATTENDANCE:

LOW ○ ○ ○ ○ ○ HIGH

ENJOYMENT:

LOW ○ ○ ○ ○ ○ HIGH

ENGAGEMENT:

LOW ○ ○ ○ ○ ○ HIGH

WHAT WAS MOST SUCCESSFUL?

WHAT COULD IMPROVE?

MEETING PLANNER

DATE:

MEETING DETAILS

TIME: .... LOCATION: .... BADGE/JOURNEY/AWARD: ....

MEETING GOAL/THEME: ....

PRE-MEETING PREP:

SUPPLIES:

- ☐
- ☐
- ☐
- ☐
- ☐

VOLUNTEERS:

- ☐
- ☐
- ☐
- ☐
- ☐

REMINDERS:

MEETING STRUCTURE:

START-UP ACTIVITY:

OPENING:

BUSINESS:

ACTIVITIES:

(1)

(2)

(3)

(4)

(5)

CLEAN-UP & CLOSING:

NEXT MEETING:

REFLECTION:

DURING THIS MEETING, THE GIRLS...

☐ DISCOVERED ☐ CONNECTED ☐ TOOK ACTION

OUR ACTIVITIES WERE...

☐ GIRL-LED ☐ HANDS-ON ☐ COOPERATIVE

ATTENDANCE:

LOW ○ ○ ○ ○ ○ HIGH

ENJOYMENT:

LOW ○ ○ ○ ○ ○ HIGH

ENGAGEMENT:

LOW ○ ○ ○ ○ ○ HIGH

WHAT WAS MOST SUCCESSFUL?

WHAT COULD IMPROVE?

MEETING PLANNER

DATE:

MEETING DETAILS

TIME: .... LOCATION: .... BADGE/JOURNEY/AWARD: ....

MEETING GOAL/THEME: ....

PRE-MEETING PREP:

SUPPLIES:

- ☐
- ☐
- ☐
- ☐
- ☐

VOLUNTEERS:

- ☐
- ☐
- ☐
- ☐
- ☐

REMINDERS:

MEETING STRUCTURE:

START-UP ACTIVITY:

OPENING:

BUSINESS:

ACTIVITIES:

(1)

(2)

(3)

(4)

(5)

CLEAN-UP & CLOSING:

NEXT MEETING:

REFLECTION:

DURING THIS MEETING, THE GIRLS...

☐ DISCOVERED ☐ CONNECTED ☐ TOOK ACTION

OUR ACTIVITIES WERE...

☐ GIRL-LED ☐ HANDS-ON ☐ COOPERATIVE

ATTENDANCE:

LOW ○ ○ ○ ○ ○ HIGH

ENJOYMENT:

LOW ○ ○ ○ ○ ○ HIGH

ENGAGEMENT:

LOW ○ ○ ○ ○ ○ HIGH

WHAT WAS MOST SUCCESSFUL?

WHAT COULD IMPROVE?

MEETING PLANNER

DATE:

MEETING DETAILS

TIME: .... LOCATION: .... BADGE/JOURNEY/AWARD: ....

MEETING GOAL/THEME: ....

PRE-MEETING PREP:

SUPPLIES:

- ☐
- ☐
- ☐
- ☐
- ☐

VOLUNTEERS:

- ☐
- ☐
- ☐
- ☐
- ☐

REMINDERS:

MEETING STRUCTURE:

START-UP ACTIVITY:

OPENING:

BUSINESS:

ACTIVITIES:

(1)

(2)

(3)

(4)

(5)

CLEAN-UP & CLOSING:

NEXT MEETING:

REFLECTION:

DURING THIS MEETING, THE GIRLS...

☐ DISCOVERED ☐ CONNECTED ☐ TOOK ACTION

OUR ACTIVITIES WERE...

☐ GIRL-LED ☐ HANDS-ON ☐ COOPERATIVE

ATTENDANCE:

LOW ◯ ◯ ◯ ◯ ◯ HIGH

ENJOYMENT:

LOW ◯ ◯ ◯ ◯ ◯ HIGH

ENGAGEMENT:

LOW ◯ ◯ ◯ ◯ ◯ HIGH

WHAT WAS MOST SUCCESSFUL?

WHAT COULD IMPROVE?

MEETING PLANNER

DATE:

MEETING DETAILS

TIME: .... LOCATION: .... BADGE/JOURNEY/AWARD: ....

MEETING GOAL/THEME: ....

PRE-MEETING PREP:

SUPPLIES:

- ☐
- ☐
- ☐
- ☐
- ☐

VOLUNTEERS:

- ☐
- ☐
- ☐
- ☐
- ☐

REMINDERS:

MEETING STRUCTURE:

START-UP ACTIVITY:

OPENING:

BUSINESS:

ACTIVITIES:

(1)

(2)

(3)

(4)

(5)

CLEAN-UP & CLOSING:

NEXT MEETING:

REFLECTION:

DURING THIS MEETING, THE GIRLS...

☐ DISCOVERED ☐ CONNECTED ☐ TOOK ACTION

OUR ACTIVITIES WERE...

☐ GIRL-LED ☐ HANDS-ON ☐ COOPERATIVE

ATTENDANCE:

LOW ○ ○ ○ ○ ○ HIGH

ENJOYMENT:

LOW ○ ○ ○ ○ ○ HIGH

ENGAGEMENT:

LOW ○ ○ ○ ○ ○ HIGH

WHAT WAS MOST SUCCESSFUL?

WHAT COULD IMPROVE?

MEETING PLANNER

DATE:

MEETING DETAILS

TIME: .... LOCATION: .... BADGE/JOURNEY/AWARD: ....

MEETING GOAL/THEME: ....

PRE-MEETING PREP:

SUPPLIES:

- ☐
- ☐
- ☐
- ☐
- ☐

VOLUNTEERS:

- ☐
- ☐
- ☐
- ☐
- ☐

REMINDERS:

MEETING STRUCTURE:

START-UP ACTIVITY:

OPENING:

BUSINESS:

ACTIVITIES:

(1)

(2)

(3)

(4)

(5)

CLEAN-UP & CLOSING:

NEXT MEETING:

REFLECTION:

DURING THIS MEETING, THE GIRLS...

☐ DISCOVERED ☐ CONNECTED ☐ TOOK ACTION

OUR ACTIVITIES WERE...

☐ GIRL-LED ☐ HANDS-ON ☐ COOPERATIVE

ATTENDANCE:

LOW ○ ○ ○ ○ ○ HIGH

ENJOYMENT:

LOW ○ ○ ○ ○ ○ HIGH

ENGAGEMENT:

LOW ○ ○ ○ ○ ○ HIGH

WHAT WAS MOST SUCCESSFUL?

WHAT COULD IMPROVE?

MEETING PLANNER

DATE:

MEETING DETAILS

TIME: .... LOCATION: .... BADGE/JOURNEY/AWARD: ....

MEETING GOAL/THEME: ....

PRE-MEETING PREP:

SUPPLIES:

☐

☐

☐

☐

☐

VOLUNTEERS:

☐

☐

☐

☐

☐

REMINDERS:

MEETING STRUCTURE:

START-UP ACTIVITY:

OPENING:

BUSINESS:

ACTIVITIES:

(1)

(2)

(3)

(4)

(5)

CLEAN-UP & CLOSING:

NEXT MEETING:

REFLECTION:

DURING THIS MEETING, THE GIRLS...

☐ DISCOVERED ☐ CONNECTED ☐ TOOK ACTION

OUR ACTIVITIES WERE...

☐ GIRL-LED ☐ HANDS-ON ☐ COOPERATIVE

ATTENDANCE:

LOW ○ ○ ○ ○ ○ HIGH

ENJOYMENT:

LOW ○ ○ ○ ○ ○ HIGH

ENGAGEMENT:

LOW ○ ○ ○ ○ ○ HIGH

WHAT WAS MOST SUCCESSFUL?

WHAT COULD IMPROVE?

MEETING PLANNER

DATE:

MEETING DETAILS

TIME: .... LOCATION: .... BADGE/JOURNEY/AWARD: ....

MEETING GOAL/THEME: ....

PRE-MEETING PREP:

SUPPLIES:

- ☐
- ☐
- ☐
- ☐
- ☐

VOLUNTEERS:

- ☐
- ☐
- ☐
- ☐
- ☐

REMINDERS:

MEETING STRUCTURE:

START-UP ACTIVITY:

OPENING:

BUSINESS:

ACTIVITIES:

(1)

(2)

(3)

(4)

(5)

CLEAN-UP & CLOSING:

NEXT MEETING:

REFLECTION:

DURING THIS MEETING, THE GIRLS...

☐ DISCOVERED ☐ CONNECTED ☐ TOOK ACTION

OUR ACTIVITIES WERE...

☐ GIRL-LED ☐ HANDS-ON ☐ COOPERATIVE

ATTENDANCE:

LOW ○ ○ ○ ○ ○ HIGH

ENJOYMENT:

LOW ○ ○ ○ ○ ○ HIGH

ENGAGEMENT:

LOW ○ ○ ○ ○ ○ HIGH

WHAT WAS MOST SUCCESSFUL?

WHAT COULD IMPROVE?

MEETING PLANNER

DATE:

MEETING DETAILS

TIME: .... LOCATION: .... BADGE/JOURNEY/AWARD: ....

MEETING GOAL/THEME: ....

PRE-MEETING PREP:

SUPPLIES:

- ☐
- ☐
- ☐
- ☐
- ☐

VOLUNTEERS:

- ☐
- ☐
- ☐
- ☐
- ☐

REMINDERS:

MEETING STRUCTURE:

START-UP ACTIVITY:

OPENING:

BUSINESS:

ACTIVITIES:

(1)

(2)

(3)

(4)

(5)

CLEAN-UP & CLOSING:

NEXT MEETING:

REFLECTION:

DURING THIS MEETING, THE GIRLS...

☐ DISCOVERED ☐ CONNECTED ☐ TOOK ACTION

OUR ACTIVITIES WERE...

☐ GIRL-LED ☐ HANDS-ON ☐ COOPERATIVE

ATTENDANCE:

LOW ○ ○ ○ ○ ○ HIGH

ENJOYMENT:

LOW ○ ○ ○ ○ ○ HIGH

ENGAGEMENT:

LOW ○ ○ ○ ○ ○ HIGH

WHAT WAS MOST SUCCESSFUL?

WHAT COULD IMPROVE?

MEETING PLANNER

DATE:

MEETING DETAILS

TIME: .... LOCATION: .... BADGE/JOURNEY/AWARD: ....

MEETING GOAL/THEME: ....

PRE-MEETING PREP:

SUPPLIES:

- ☐
- ☐
- ☐
- ☐
- ☐

VOLUNTEERS:

- ☐
- ☐
- ☐
- ☐
- ☐

REMINDERS:

MEETING STRUCTURE:

START-UP ACTIVITY:

OPENING:

BUSINESS:

ACTIVITIES:

(1)

(2)

(3)

(4)

(5)

CLEAN-UP & CLOSING:

NEXT MEETING:

REFLECTION:

DURING THIS MEETING, THE GIRLS...

☐ DISCOVERED ☐ CONNECTED ☐ TOOK ACTION

OUR ACTIVITIES WERE...

☐ GIRL-LED ☐ HANDS-ON ☐ COOPERATIVE

ATTENDANCE:

LOW ○ ○ ○ ○ ○ HIGH

ENJOYMENT:

LOW ○ ○ ○ ○ ○ HIGH

ENGAGEMENT:

LOW ○ ○ ○ ○ ○ HIGH

WHAT WAS MOST SUCCESSFUL?

WHAT COULD IMPROVE?

MEETING PLANNER

DATE:

MEETING DETAILS

TIME: .... LOCATION: .... BADGE/JOURNEY/AWARD: ....

MEETING GOAL/THEME: ....

PRE-MEETING PREP:

SUPPLIES:

☐
☐
☐
☐
☐

VOLUNTEERS:

☐
☐
☐
☐
☐

REMINDERS:

MEETING STRUCTURE:

START-UP ACTIVITY:

OPENING:

BUSINESS:

ACTIVITIES:

(1)

(2)

(3)

(4)

(5)

CLEAN-UP & CLOSING:

NEXT MEETING:

REFLECTION:

DURING THIS MEETING, THE GIRLS...

☐ DISCOVERED ☐ CONNECTED ☐ TOOK ACTION

OUR ACTIVITIES WERE...

☐ GIRL-LED ☐ HANDS-ON ☐ COOPERATIVE

ATTENDANCE:

LOW ○ ○ ○ ○ ○ HIGH

ENJOYMENT:

LOW ○ ○ ○ ○ ○ HIGH

ENGAGEMENT:

LOW ○ ○ ○ ○ ○ HIGH

WHAT WAS MOST SUCCESSFUL?

WHAT COULD IMPROVE?

MEETING PLANNER

DATE:

MEETING DETAILS

TIME: .... LOCATION: .... BADGE/JOURNEY/AWARD: ....

MEETING GOAL/THEME: ....

PRE-MEETING PREP:

SUPPLIES:

- ☐
- ☐
- ☐
- ☐
- ☐

VOLUNTEERS:

- ☐
- ☐
- ☐
- ☐
- ☐

REMINDERS:

MEETING STRUCTURE:

START-UP ACTIVITY:

OPENING:

BUSINESS:

ACTIVITIES:

(1)

(2)

(3)

(4)

(5)

CLEAN-UP & CLOSING:

NEXT MEETING:

REFLECTION:

DURING THIS MEETING, THE GIRLS...

☐ DISCOVERED ☐ CONNECTED ☐ TOOK ACTION

OUR ACTIVITIES WERE...

☐ GIRL-LED ☐ HANDS-ON ☐ COOPERATIVE

ATTENDANCE:

LOW ○ ○ ○ ○ ○ HIGH

ENJOYMENT:

LOW ○ ○ ○ ○ ○ HIGH

ENGAGEMENT:

LOW ○ ○ ○ ○ ○ HIGH

WHAT WAS MOST SUCCESSFUL?

WHAT COULD IMPROVE?

MEETING PLANNER

DATE:

MEETING DETAILS

TIME: .... LOCATION: .... BADGE/JOURNEY/AWARD: ....

MEETING GOAL/THEME: ....

PRE-MEETING PREP:

SUPPLIES:

- ☐
- ☐
- ☐
- ☐
- ☐

VOLUNTEERS:

- ☐
- ☐
- ☐
- ☐
- ☐

REMINDERS:

MEETING STRUCTURE:

START-UP ACTIVITY:

OPENING:

BUSINESS:

ACTIVITIES:

(1)

(2)

(3)

(4)

(5)

CLEAN-UP & CLOSING:

NEXT MEETING:

REFLECTION:

DURING THIS MEETING, THE GIRLS...

☐ DISCOVERED ☐ CONNECTED ☐ TOOK ACTION

OUR ACTIVITIES WERE...

☐ GIRL-LED ☐ HANDS-ON ☐ COOPERATIVE

ATTENDANCE:

LOW ○ ○ ○ ○ ○ HIGH

ENJOYMENT:

LOW ○ ○ ○ ○ ○ HIGH

ENGAGEMENT:

LOW ○ ○ ○ ○ ○ HIGH

WHAT WAS MOST SUCCESSFUL?

WHAT COULD IMPROVE?

MEETING PLANNER

DATE:

MEETING DETAILS

TIME: .... LOCATION: .... BADGE/JOURNEY/AWARD: ....

MEETING GOAL/THEME: ....

PRE-MEETING PREP:

SUPPLIES:

- ☐
- ☐
- ☐
- ☐
- ☐

VOLUNTEERS:

- ☐
- ☐
- ☐
- ☐
- ☐

REMINDERS:

MEETING STRUCTURE:

START-UP ACTIVITY:

OPENING:

BUSINESS:

ACTIVITIES:

(1)

(2)

(3)

(4)

(5)

CLEAN-UP & CLOSING:

NEXT MEETING:

REFLECTION:

DURING THIS MEETING, THE GIRLS...

☐ DISCOVERED ☐ CONNECTED ☐ TOOK ACTION

OUR ACTIVITIES WERE...

☐ GIRL-LED ☐ HANDS-ON ☐ COOPERATIVE

ATTENDANCE:

LOW ○ ○ ○ ○ ○ HIGH

ENJOYMENT:

LOW ○ ○ ○ ○ ○ HIGH

ENGAGEMENT:

LOW ○ ○ ○ ○ ○ HIGH

WHAT WAS MOST SUCCESSFUL?

WHAT COULD IMPROVE?

MEETING PLANNER

DATE:

MEETING DETAILS

TIME: .... LOCATION: .... BADGE/JOURNEY/AWARD: ....

MEETING GOAL/THEME: ....

PRE-MEETING PREP:

SUPPLIES:

- ☐
- ☐
- ☐
- ☐
- ☐

VOLUNTEERS:

- ☐
- ☐
- ☐
- ☐
- ☐

REMINDERS:

MEETING STRUCTURE:

START-UP ACTIVITY:

OPENING:

BUSINESS:

ACTIVITIES:

(1)

(2)

(3)

(4)

(5)

CLEAN-UP & CLOSING:

NEXT MEETING:

REFLECTION:

DURING THIS MEETING, THE GIRLS...

☐ DISCOVERED ☐ CONNECTED ☐ TOOK ACTION

OUR ACTIVITIES WERE...

☐ GIRL-LED ☐ HANDS-ON ☐ COOPERATIVE

ATTENDANCE:

LOW ○ ○ ○ ○ ○ HIGH

ENJOYMENT:

LOW ○ ○ ○ ○ ○ HIGH

ENGAGEMENT:

LOW ○ ○ ○ ○ ○ HIGH

WHAT WAS MOST SUCCESSFUL?

WHAT COULD IMPROVE?

MEETING PLANNER

DATE:

MEETING DETAILS

TIME: .... LOCATION: .... BADGE/JOURNEY/AWARD: ....

MEETING GOAL/THEME: ....

PRE-MEETING PREP:

SUPPLIES:

- ☐
- ☐
- ☐
- ☐
- ☐

VOLUNTEERS:

- ☐
- ☐
- ☐
- ☐
- ☐

REMINDERS:

MEETING STRUCTURE:

START-UP ACTIVITY:

OPENING:

BUSINESS:

ACTIVITIES:

(1)

(2)

(3)

(4)

(5)

CLEAN-UP & CLOSING:

NEXT MEETING:

REFLECTION:

DURING THIS MEETING, THE GIRLS...

☐ DISCOVERED ☐ CONNECTED ☐ TOOK ACTION

OUR ACTIVITIES WERE...

☐ GIRL-LED ☐ HANDS-ON ☐ COOPERATIVE

ATTENDANCE:

LOW ○ ○ ○ ○ ○ HIGH

ENJOYMENT:

LOW ○ ○ ○ ○ ○ HIGH

ENGAGEMENT:

LOW ○ ○ ○ ○ ○ HIGH

WHAT WAS MOST SUCCESSFUL?

WHAT COULD IMPROVE?

MEETING PLANNER

DATE:

MEETING DETAILS

TIME: .... LOCATION: .... BADGE/JOURNEY/AWARD: ....

MEETING GOAL/THEME: ....

PRE-MEETING PREP:

SUPPLIES:

- ☐
- ☐
- ☐
- ☐
- ☐

VOLUNTEERS:

- ☐
- ☐
- ☐
- ☐
- ☐

REMINDERS:

MEETING STRUCTURE:

START-UP ACTIVITY:

OPENING:

BUSINESS:

ACTIVITIES:

(1)

(2)

(3)

(4)

(5)

CLEAN-UP & CLOSING:

NEXT MEETING:

REFLECTION:

DURING THIS MEETING, THE GIRLS...

☐ DISCOVERED ☐ CONNECTED ☐ TOOK ACTION

OUR ACTIVITIES WERE...

☐ GIRL-LED ☐ HANDS-ON ☐ COOPERATIVE

ATTENDANCE:

LOW ○ ○ ○ ○ ○ HIGH

ENJOYMENT:

LOW ○ ○ ○ ○ ○ HIGH

ENGAGEMENT:

LOW ○ ○ ○ ○ ○ HIGH

WHAT WAS MOST SUCCESSFUL?

WHAT COULD IMPROVE?

MEETING PLANNER

DATE:

MEETING DETAILS

TIME: .... LOCATION: .... BADGE/JOURNEY/AWARD: ....

MEETING GOAL/THEME: ....

PRE-MEETING PREP:

SUPPLIES:

- ☐
- ☐
- ☐
- ☐
- ☐

VOLUNTEERS:

- ☐
- ☐
- ☐
- ☐
- ☐

REMINDERS:

MEETING STRUCTURE:

START-UP ACTIVITY:

OPENING:

BUSINESS:

ACTIVITIES:

(1)

(2)

(3)

(4)

(5)

CLEAN-UP & CLOSING:

NEXT MEETING:

REFLECTION:

DURING THIS MEETING, THE GIRLS...

☐ DISCOVERED ☐ CONNECTED ☐ TOOK ACTION

OUR ACTIVITIES WERE...

☐ GIRL-LED ☐ HANDS-ON ☐ COOPERATIVE

ATTENDANCE:

LOW ○ ○ ○ ○ ○ HIGH

ENJOYMENT:

LOW ○ ○ ○ ○ ○ HIGH

ENGAGEMENT:

LOW ○ ○ ○ ○ ○ HIGH

WHAT WAS MOST SUCCESSFUL?

WHAT COULD IMPROVE?

MEETING PLANNER

DATE:

MEETING DETAILS

TIME: .... LOCATION: .... BADGE/JOURNEY/AWARD: ....

MEETING GOAL/THEME: ....

PRE-MEETING PREP:

SUPPLIES:

- ☐
- ☐
- ☐
- ☐
- ☐

VOLUNTEERS:

- ☐
- ☐
- ☐
- ☐
- ☐

REMINDERS:

MEETING STRUCTURE:

START-UP ACTIVITY:

OPENING:

BUSINESS:

ACTIVITIES:

(1)

(2)

(3)

(4)

(5)

CLEAN-UP & CLOSING:

NEXT MEETING:

REFLECTION:

DURING THIS MEETING, THE GIRLS...

☐ DISCOVERED ☐ CONNECTED ☐ TOOK ACTION

OUR ACTIVITIES WERE...

☐ GIRL-LED ☐ HANDS-ON ☐ COOPERATIVE

ATTENDANCE:

LOW ○ ○ ○ ○ ○ HIGH

ENJOYMENT:

LOW ○ ○ ○ ○ ○ HIGH

ENGAGEMENT:

LOW ○ ○ ○ ○ ○ HIGH

WHAT WAS MOST SUCCESSFUL?

WHAT COULD IMPROVE?

MEETING PLANNER

DATE:

MEETING DETAILS

TIME: .... LOCATION: .... BADGE/JOURNEY/AWARD: ....

MEETING GOAL/THEME: ....

PRE-MEETING PREP:

SUPPLIES:

- ☐
- ☐
- ☐
- ☐
- ☐

VOLUNTEERS:

- ☐
- ☐
- ☐
- ☐
- ☐

REMINDERS:

MEETING STRUCTURE:

START-UP ACTIVITY:

OPENING:

BUSINESS:

ACTIVITIES:

(1)

(2)

(3)

(4)

(5)

CLEAN-UP & CLOSING:

NEXT MEETING:

REFLECTION:

DURING THIS MEETING, THE GIRLS...

☐ DISCOVERED ☐ CONNECTED ☐ TOOK ACTION

OUR ACTIVITIES WERE...

☐ GIRL-LED ☐ HANDS-ON ☐ COOPERATIVE

ATTENDANCE:

LOW ○ ○ ○ ○ ○ HIGH

ENJOYMENT:

LOW ○ ○ ○ ○ ○ HIGH

ENGAGEMENT:

LOW ○ ○ ○ ○ ○ HIGH

WHAT WAS MOST SUCCESSFUL?

WHAT COULD IMPROVE?

MEETING PLANNER

DATE:

MEETING DETAILS

TIME: .... LOCATION: .... BADGE/JOURNEY/AWARD: ....

MEETING GOAL/THEME: ....

PRE-MEETING PREP:

SUPPLIES:

- ☐
- ☐
- ☐
- ☐
- ☐

VOLUNTEERS:

- ☐
- ☐
- ☐
- ☐
- ☐

REMINDERS:

MEETING STRUCTURE:

START-UP ACTIVITY:

OPENING:

BUSINESS:

ACTIVITIES:

(1)

(2)

(3)

(4)

(5)

CLEAN-UP & CLOSING:

NEXT MEETING:

REFLECTION:

DURING THIS MEETING, THE GIRLS...

☐ DISCOVERED ☐ CONNECTED ☐ TOOK ACTION

OUR ACTIVITIES WERE...

☐ GIRL-LED ☐ HANDS-ON ☐ COOPERATIVE

ATTENDANCE:

LOW ○ ○ ○ ○ ○ HIGH

ENJOYMENT:

LOW ○ ○ ○ ○ ○ HIGH

ENGAGEMENT:

LOW ○ ○ ○ ○ ○ HIGH

WHAT WAS MOST SUCCESSFUL?

WHAT COULD IMPROVE?

MEETING PLANNER

DATE:

MEETING DETAILS

TIME: .... LOCATION: .... BADGE/JOURNEY/AWARD: ....

MEETING GOAL/THEME: ....

PRE-MEETING PREP:

SUPPLIES:

- ☐
- ☐
- ☐
- ☐
- ☐

VOLUNTEERS:

- ☐
- ☐
- ☐
- ☐
- ☐

REMINDERS:

MEETING STRUCTURE:

START-UP ACTIVITY:

OPENING:

BUSINESS:

ACTIVITIES:

(1)

(2)

(3)

(4)

(5)

CLEAN-UP & CLOSING:

NEXT MEETING:

REFLECTION:

DURING THIS MEETING, THE GIRLS...

☐ DISCOVERED ☐ CONNECTED ☐ TOOK ACTION

OUR ACTIVITIES WERE...

☐ GIRL-LED ☐ HANDS-ON ☐ COOPERATIVE

ATTENDANCE:

LOW ○ ○ ○ ○ ○ HIGH

ENJOYMENT:

LOW ○ ○ ○ ○ ○ HIGH

ENGAGEMENT:

LOW ○ ○ ○ ○ ○ HIGH

WHAT WAS MOST SUCCESSFUL?

WHAT COULD IMPROVE?

MEETING PLANNER

DATE:

MEETING DETAILS

TIME: .... LOCATION: .... BADGE/JOURNEY/AWARD: ....

MEETING GOAL/THEME: ....

PRE-MEETING PREP:

SUPPLIES:

- ☐
- ☐
- ☐
- ☐
- ☐

VOLUNTEERS:

- ☐
- ☐
- ☐
- ☐
- ☐

REMINDERS:

MEETING STRUCTURE:

START-UP ACTIVITY:

OPENING:

BUSINESS:

ACTIVITIES:

(1)

(2)

(3)

(4)

(5)

CLEAN-UP & CLOSING:

NEXT MEETING:

REFLECTION:

DURING THIS MEETING, THE GIRLS...

☐ DISCOVERED ☐ CONNECTED ☐ TOOK ACTION

OUR ACTIVITIES WERE...

☐ GIRL-LED ☐ HANDS-ON ☐ COOPERATIVE

ATTENDANCE:

LOW ○ ○ ○ ○ ○ HIGH

ENJOYMENT:

LOW ○ ○ ○ ○ ○ HIGH

ENGAGEMENT:

LOW ○ ○ ○ ○ ○ HIGH

WHAT WAS MOST SUCCESSFUL?

WHAT COULD IMPROVE?

MEETING PLANNER

DATE:

MEETING DETAILS

TIME: .... LOCATION: .... BADGE/JOURNEY/AWARD: ....

MEETING GOAL/THEME: ....

PRE-MEETING PREP:

SUPPLIES:

☐
☐
☐
☐
☐

VOLUNTEERS:

☐
☐
☐
☐
☐

REMINDERS:

MEETING STRUCTURE:

START-UP ACTIVITY:

OPENING:

BUSINESS:

ACTIVITIES:

(1)

(2)

(3)

(4)

(5)

CLEAN-UP & CLOSING:

NEXT MEETING:

REFLECTION:

DURING THIS MEETING, THE GIRLS...

☐ DISCOVERED ☐ CONNECTED ☐ TOOK ACTION

OUR ACTIVITIES WERE...

☐ GIRL-LED ☐ HANDS-ON ☐ COOPERATIVE

ATTENDANCE:

LOW ○ ○ ○ ○ ○ HIGH

ENJOYMENT:

LOW ○ ○ ○ ○ ○ HIGH

ENGAGEMENT:

LOW ○ ○ ○ ○ ○ HIGH

WHAT WAS MOST SUCCESSFUL?

WHAT COULD IMPROVE?

MEETING PLANNER

DATE:

MEETING DETAILS

TIME: .... LOCATION: .... BADGE/JOURNEY/AWARD: ....

MEETING GOAL/THEME: ....

PRE-MEETING PREP:

SUPPLIES:

- ☐
- ☐
- ☐
- ☐
- ☐

VOLUNTEERS:

- ☐
- ☐
- ☐
- ☐
- ☐

REMINDERS:

MEETING STRUCTURE:

START-UP ACTIVITY:

OPENING:

BUSINESS:

ACTIVITIES:

(1)

(2)

(3)

(4)

(5)

CLEAN-UP & CLOSING:

NEXT MEETING:

REFLECTION:

DURING THIS MEETING, THE GIRLS...

☐ DISCOVERED ☐ CONNECTED ☐ TOOK ACTION

OUR ACTIVITIES WERE...

☐ GIRL-LED ☐ HANDS-ON ☐ COOPERATIVE

ATTENDANCE:

LOW ○ ○ ○ ○ ○ HIGH

ENJOYMENT:

LOW ○ ○ ○ ○ ○ HIGH

ENGAGEMENT:

LOW ○ ○ ○ ○ ○ HIGH

WHAT WAS MOST SUCCESSFUL?

WHAT COULD IMPROVE?

MEETING PLANNER

DATE:

MEETING DETAILS

TIME: .... LOCATION: .... BADGE/JOURNEY/AWARD: ....

MEETING GOAL/THEME: ....

PRE-MEETING PREP:

SUPPLIES:

- ☐
- ☐
- ☐
- ☐
- ☐

VOLUNTEERS:

- ☐
- ☐
- ☐
- ☐
- ☐

REMINDERS:

MEETING STRUCTURE:

START-UP ACTIVITY:

OPENING:

BUSINESS:

ACTIVITIES:

(1)

(2)

(3)

(4)

(5)

CLEAN-UP & CLOSING:

NEXT MEETING:

REFLECTION:

DURING THIS MEETING, THE GIRLS...

☐ DISCOVERED ☐ CONNECTED ☐ TOOK ACTION

OUR ACTIVITIES WERE...

☐ GIRL-LED ☐ HANDS-ON ☐ COOPERATIVE

ATTENDANCE:

LOW ○ ○ ○ ○ ○ HIGH

ENJOYMENT:

LOW ○ ○ ○ ○ ○ HIGH

ENGAGEMENT:

LOW ○ ○ ○ ○ ○ HIGH

WHAT WAS MOST SUCCESSFUL?

WHAT COULD IMPROVE?

BADGE ACTIVITIES PLANNER

BADGE:

PURPOSE: ....

OF MEETINGS TO COMPLETE THIS BADGE: .... JOURNEY CONNECTION(S): .... ☐ STEP 1 ☐ STEP 2 ☐ STEP 3 ☐ STEP 4 ☐ STEP 5

LONG-TERM PLANNING:

FIELD TRIP/GUEST SPEAKER IDEAS:

STEP 1: TIME NEEDED: .... MINUTES

ACTIVITY: .... TO BE COMPLETED AT: ☐ HOME ☐ MEETING ☐ EVENT ☐ FIELD TRIP

PREP/SUPPLIES NEEDED: WHO'S RESPONSIBLE?

(1) .... ☐ LEADER ☐ GIRL/VOLUNTEER: ....

(2) .... ☐ LEADER ☐ GIRL/VOLUNTEER: ....

(3) .... ☐ LEADER ☐ GIRL/VOLUNTEER: ....

(4) .... ☐ LEADER ☐ GIRL/VOLUNTEER: ....

(5) .... ☐ LEADER ☐ GIRL/VOLUNTEER: ....

ACTIVITY STEPS/NOTES:

LEADERSHIP KEYS: ☐ DISCOVER ☐ CONNECT ☐ TAKE ACTION PROCESSES: ☐ GIRL-LED ☐ LEARNING BY DOING ☐ COOPERATIVE LEARNING

STEP 2: TIME NEEDED: .... MINUTES

ACTIVITY: .... TO BE COMPLETED AT: ☐ HOME ☐ MEETING ☐ EVENT ☐ FIELD TRIP

PREP/SUPPLIES NEEDED: WHO'S RESPONSIBLE?

(1) .... ☐ LEADER ☐ GIRL/VOLUNTEER: ....

(2) .... ☐ LEADER ☐ GIRL/VOLUNTEER: ....

(3) .... ☐ LEADER ☐ GIRL/VOLUNTEER: ....

(4) .... ☐ LEADER ☐ GIRL/VOLUNTEER: ....

(5) .... ☐ LEADER ☐ GIRL/VOLUNTEER: ....

ACTIVITY STEPS/NOTES:

LEADERSHIP KEYS: ☐ DISCOVER ☐ CONNECT ☐ TAKE ACTION PROCESSES: ☐ GIRL-LED ☐ LEARNING BY DOING ☐ COOPERATIVE LEARNING

STEP 3:

TIME NEEDED: .... MINUTES

ACTIVITY: .... TO BE COMPLETED AT: ☐ HOME ☐ MEETING ☐ EVENT ☐ FIELD TRIP

PREP/SUPPLIES NEEDED: WHO'S RESPONSIBLE?

(1) .... ☐ LEADER ☐ GIRL/VOLUNTEER: ....

(2) .... ☐ LEADER ☐ GIRL/VOLUNTEER: ....

(3) .... ☐ LEADER ☐ GIRL/VOLUNTEER: ....

(4) .... ☐ LEADER ☐ GIRL/VOLUNTEER: ....

(5) .... ☐ LEADER ☐ GIRL/VOLUNTEER: ....

ACTIVITY STEPS/NOTES:

LEADERSHIP KEYS: ☐ DISCOVER ☐ CONNECT ☐ TAKE ACTION PROCESSES: ☐ GIRL-LED ☐ LEARNING BY DOING ☐ COOPERATIVE LEARNING

STEP 4:

TIME NEEDED: .... MINUTES

ACTIVITY: .... TO BE COMPLETED AT: ☐ HOME ☐ MEETING ☐ EVENT ☐ FIELD TRIP

PREP/SUPPLIES NEEDED: WHO'S RESPONSIBLE?

(1) .... ☐ LEADER ☐ GIRL/VOLUNTEER: ....

(2) .... ☐ LEADER ☐ GIRL/VOLUNTEER: ....

(3) .... ☐ LEADER ☐ GIRL/VOLUNTEER: ....

(4) .... ☐ LEADER ☐ GIRL/VOLUNTEER: ....

(5) .... ☐ LEADER ☐ GIRL/VOLUNTEER: ....

ACTIVITY STEPS/NOTES:

LEADERSHIP KEYS: ☐ DISCOVER ☐ CONNECT ☐ TAKE ACTION PROCESSES: ☐ GIRL-LED ☐ LEARNING BY DOING ☐ COOPERATIVE LEARNING

STEP 5:

TIME NEEDED: .... MINUTES

ACTIVITY: .... TO BE COMPLETED AT: ☐ HOME ☐ MEETING ☐ EVENT ☐ FIELD TRIP

PREP/SUPPLIES NEEDED: WHO'S RESPONSIBLE?

(1) .... ☐ LEADER ☐ GIRL/VOLUNTEER: ....

(2) .... ☐ LEADER ☐ GIRL/VOLUNTEER: ....

(3) .... ☐ LEADER ☐ GIRL/VOLUNTEER: ....

(4) .... ☐ LEADER ☐ GIRL/VOLUNTEER: ....

(5) .... ☐ LEADER ☐ GIRL/VOLUNTEER: ....

ACTIVITY STEPS/NOTES:

LEADERSHIP KEYS: ☐ DISCOVER ☐ CONNECT ☐ TAKE ACTION PROCESSES: ☐ GIRL-LED ☐ LEARNING BY DOING ☐ COOPERATIVE LEARNING

BADGE ACTIVITIES PLANNER

BADGE:

PURPOSE: ....

OF MEETINGS TO COMPLETE THIS BADGE: .... JOURNEY CONNECTION(S): .... ☐ STEP 1 ☐ STEP 2 ☐ STEP 3 ☐ STEP 4 ☐ STEP 5

LONG-TERM PLANNING:

FIELD TRIP/GUEST SPEAKER IDEAS:

STEP 1:

TIME NEEDED: .... MINUTES

ACTIVITY: .... TO BE COMPLETED AT: ☐ HOME ☐ MEETING ☐ EVENT ☐ FIELD TRIP

PREP/SUPPLIES NEEDED:

WHO'S RESPONSIBLE?

(1) .... ☐ LEADER ☐ GIRL/VOLUNTEER: ....

(2) .... ☐ LEADER ☐ GIRL/VOLUNTEER: ....

(3) .... ☐ LEADER ☐ GIRL/VOLUNTEER: ....

(4) .... ☐ LEADER ☐ GIRL/VOLUNTEER: ....

(5) .... ☐ LEADER ☐ GIRL/VOLUNTEER: ....

ACTIVITY STEPS/NOTES:

LEADERSHIP KEYS: ☐ DISCOVER ☐ CONNECT ☐ TAKE ACTION PROCESSES: ☐ GIRL-LED ☐ LEARNING BY DOING ☐ COOPERATIVE LEARNING

STEP 2:

TIME NEEDED: .... MINUTES

ACTIVITY: .... TO BE COMPLETED AT: ☐ HOME ☐ MEETING ☐ EVENT ☐ FIELD TRIP

PREP/SUPPLIES NEEDED:

WHO'S RESPONSIBLE?

(1) .... ☐ LEADER ☐ GIRL/VOLUNTEER: ....

(2) .... ☐ LEADER ☐ GIRL/VOLUNTEER: ....

(3) .... ☐ LEADER ☐ GIRL/VOLUNTEER: ....

(4) .... ☐ LEADER ☐ GIRL/VOLUNTEER: ....

(5) .... ☐ LEADER ☐ GIRL/VOLUNTEER: ....

ACTIVITY STEPS/NOTES:

LEADERSHIP KEYS: ☐ DISCOVER ☐ CONNECT ☐ TAKE ACTION PROCESSES: ☐ GIRL-LED ☐ LEARNING BY DOING ☐ COOPERATIVE LEARNING

STEP 3:

TIME NEEDED: .... MINUTES

ACTIVITY: .... TO BE COMPLETED AT: ☐ HOME ☐ MEETING ☐ EVENT ☐ FIELD TRIP

PREP/SUPPLIES NEEDED: WHO'S RESPONSIBLE?

(1) .... ☐ LEADER ☐ GIRL/VOLUNTEER: ....

(2) .... ☐ LEADER ☐ GIRL/VOLUNTEER: ....

(3) .... ☐ LEADER ☐ GIRL/VOLUNTEER: ....

(4) .... ☐ LEADER ☐ GIRL/VOLUNTEER: ....

(5) .... ☐ LEADER ☐ GIRL/VOLUNTEER: ....

ACTIVITY STEPS/NOTES:

LEADERSHIP KEYS: ☐ DISCOVER ☐ CONNECT ☐ TAKE ACTION PROCESSES: ☐ GIRL-LED ☐ LEARNING BY DOING ☐ COOPERATIVE LEARNING

STEP 4:

TIME NEEDED: .... MINUTES

ACTIVITY: .... TO BE COMPLETED AT: ☐ HOME ☐ MEETING ☐ EVENT ☐ FIELD TRIP

PREP/SUPPLIES NEEDED: WHO'S RESPONSIBLE?

(1) .... ☐ LEADER ☐ GIRL/VOLUNTEER: ....

(2) .... ☐ LEADER ☐ GIRL/VOLUNTEER: ....

(3) .... ☐ LEADER ☐ GIRL/VOLUNTEER: ....

(4) .... ☐ LEADER ☐ GIRL/VOLUNTEER: ....

(5) .... ☐ LEADER ☐ GIRL/VOLUNTEER: ....

ACTIVITY STEPS/NOTES:

LEADERSHIP KEYS: ☐ DISCOVER ☐ CONNECT ☐ TAKE ACTION PROCESSES: ☐ GIRL-LED ☐ LEARNING BY DOING ☐ COOPERATIVE LEARNING

STEP 5:

TIME NEEDED: .... MINUTES

ACTIVITY: .... TO BE COMPLETED AT: ☐ HOME ☐ MEETING ☐ EVENT ☐ FIELD TRIP

PREP/SUPPLIES NEEDED: WHO'S RESPONSIBLE?

(1) .... ☐ LEADER ☐ GIRL/VOLUNTEER: ....

(2) .... ☐ LEADER ☐ GIRL/VOLUNTEER: ....

(3) .... ☐ LEADER ☐ GIRL/VOLUNTEER: ....

(4) .... ☐ LEADER ☐ GIRL/VOLUNTEER: ....

(5) .... ☐ LEADER ☐ GIRL/VOLUNTEER: ....

ACTIVITY STEPS/NOTES:

LEADERSHIP KEYS: ☐ DISCOVER ☐ CONNECT ☐ TAKE ACTION PROCESSES: ☐ GIRL-LED ☐ LEARNING BY DOING ☐ COOPERATIVE LEARNING

BADGE ACTIVITIES PLANNER

BADGE:

PURPOSE: ....

OF MEETINGS TO COMPLETE THIS BADGE: .... JOURNEY CONNECTION(S): .... ☐ STEP 1 ☐ STEP 2 ☐ STEP 3 ☐ STEP 4 ☐ STEP 5

LONG-TERM PLANNING:

FIELD TRIP/GUEST SPEAKER IDEAS:

STEP 1: TIME NEEDED: .... MINUTES

ACTIVITY: .... TO BE COMPLETED AT: ☐ HOME ☐ MEETING ☐ EVENT ☐ FIELD TRIP

PREP/SUPPLIES NEEDED: WHO'S RESPONSIBLE?

(1) .... ☐ LEADER ☐ GIRL/VOLUNTEER: ....

(2) .... ☐ LEADER ☐ GIRL/VOLUNTEER: ....

(3) .... ☐ LEADER ☐ GIRL/VOLUNTEER: ....

(4) .... ☐ LEADER ☐ GIRL/VOLUNTEER: ....

(5) .... ☐ LEADER ☐ GIRL/VOLUNTEER: ....

ACTIVITY STEPS/NOTES:

LEADERSHIP KEYS: ☐ DISCOVER ☐ CONNECT ☐ TAKE ACTION PROCESSES: ☐ GIRL-LED ☐ LEARNING BY DOING ☐ COOPERATIVE LEARNING

STEP 2: TIME NEEDED: .... MINUTES

ACTIVITY: .... TO BE COMPLETED AT: ☐ HOME ☐ MEETING ☐ EVENT ☐ FIELD TRIP

PREP/SUPPLIES NEEDED: WHO'S RESPONSIBLE?

(1) .... ☐ LEADER ☐ GIRL/VOLUNTEER: ....

(2) .... ☐ LEADER ☐ GIRL/VOLUNTEER: ....

(3) .... ☐ LEADER ☐ GIRL/VOLUNTEER: ....

(4) .... ☐ LEADER ☐ GIRL/VOLUNTEER: ....

(5) .... ☐ LEADER ☐ GIRL/VOLUNTEER: ....

ACTIVITY STEPS/NOTES:

LEADERSHIP KEYS: ☐ DISCOVER ☐ CONNECT ☐ TAKE ACTION PROCESSES: ☐ GIRL-LED ☐ LEARNING BY DOING ☐ COOPERATIVE LEARNING

STEP 3:

TIME NEEDED: .... MINUTES

ACTIVITY: .... TO BE COMPLETED AT: ☐ HOME ☐ MEETING ☐ EVENT ☐ FIELD TRIP

PREP/SUPPLIES NEEDED: WHO'S RESPONSIBLE?

(1) .... ☐ LEADER ☐ GIRL/VOLUNTEER: ....

(2) .... ☐ LEADER ☐ GIRL/VOLUNTEER: ....

(3) .... ☐ LEADER ☐ GIRL/VOLUNTEER: ....

(4) .... ☐ LEADER ☐ GIRL/VOLUNTEER: ....

(5) .... ☐ LEADER ☐ GIRL/VOLUNTEER: ....

ACTIVITY STEPS/NOTES:

LEADERSHIP KEYS: ☐ DISCOVER ☐ CONNECT ☐ TAKE ACTION PROCESSES: ☐ GIRL-LED ☐ LEARNING BY DOING ☐ COOPERATIVE LEARNING

STEP 4:

TIME NEEDED: .... MINUTES

ACTIVITY: .... TO BE COMPLETED AT: ☐ HOME ☐ MEETING ☐ EVENT ☐ FIELD TRIP

PREP/SUPPLIES NEEDED: WHO'S RESPONSIBLE?

(1) .... ☐ LEADER ☐ GIRL/VOLUNTEER: ....

(2) .... ☐ LEADER ☐ GIRL/VOLUNTEER: ....

(3) .... ☐ LEADER ☐ GIRL/VOLUNTEER: ....

(4) .... ☐ LEADER ☐ GIRL/VOLUNTEER: ....

(5) .... ☐ LEADER ☐ GIRL/VOLUNTEER: ....

ACTIVITY STEPS/NOTES:

LEADERSHIP KEYS: ☐ DISCOVER ☐ CONNECT ☐ TAKE ACTION PROCESSES: ☐ GIRL-LED ☐ LEARNING BY DOING ☐ COOPERATIVE LEARNING

STEP 5:

TIME NEEDED: .... MINUTES

ACTIVITY: .... TO BE COMPLETED AT: ☐ HOME ☐ MEETING ☐ EVENT ☐ FIELD TRIP

PREP/SUPPLIES NEEDED: WHO'S RESPONSIBLE?

(1) .... ☐ LEADER ☐ GIRL/VOLUNTEER: ....

(2) .... ☐ LEADER ☐ GIRL/VOLUNTEER: ....

(3) .... ☐ LEADER ☐ GIRL/VOLUNTEER: ....

(4) .... ☐ LEADER ☐ GIRL/VOLUNTEER: ....

(5) .... ☐ LEADER ☐ GIRL/VOLUNTEER: ....

ACTIVITY STEPS/NOTES:

LEADERSHIP KEYS: ☐ DISCOVER ☐ CONNECT ☐ TAKE ACTION PROCESSES: ☐ GIRL-LED ☐ LEARNING BY DOING ☐ COOPERATIVE LEARNING

BADGE ACTIVITIES PLANNER

BADGE:

PURPOSE: ....

OF MEETINGS TO COMPLETE THIS BADGE: .... JOURNEY CONNECTION(S): .... ☐ STEP 1 ☐ STEP 2 ☐ STEP 3 ☐ STEP 4 ☐ STEP 5

LONG-TERM PLANNING:

FIELD TRIP/GUEST SPEAKER IDEAS:

STEP 1:

TIME NEEDED: .... MINUTES

ACTIVITY: .... TO BE COMPLETED AT: ☐ HOME ☐ MEETING ☐ EVENT ☐ FIELD TRIP

PREP/SUPPLIES NEEDED: WHO'S RESPONSIBLE?

(1) .... ☐ LEADER ☐ GIRL/VOLUNTEER: ....

(2) .... ☐ LEADER ☐ GIRL/VOLUNTEER: ....

(3) .... ☐ LEADER ☐ GIRL/VOLUNTEER: ....

(4) .... ☐ LEADER ☐ GIRL/VOLUNTEER: ....

(5) .... ☐ LEADER ☐ GIRL/VOLUNTEER: ....

ACTIVITY STEPS/NOTES:

LEADERSHIP KEYS: ☐ DISCOVER ☐ CONNECT ☐ TAKE ACTION PROCESSES: ☐ GIRL-LED ☐ LEARNING BY DOING ☐ COOPERATIVE LEARNING

STEP 2:

TIME NEEDED: .... MINUTES

ACTIVITY: .... TO BE COMPLETED AT: ☐ HOME ☐ MEETING ☐ EVENT ☐ FIELD TRIP

PREP/SUPPLIES NEEDED: WHO'S RESPONSIBLE?

(1) .... ☐ LEADER ☐ GIRL/VOLUNTEER: ....

(2) .... ☐ LEADER ☐ GIRL/VOLUNTEER: ....

(3) .... ☐ LEADER ☐ GIRL/VOLUNTEER: ....

(4) .... ☐ LEADER ☐ GIRL/VOLUNTEER: ....

(5) .... ☐ LEADER ☐ GIRL/VOLUNTEER: ....

ACTIVITY STEPS/NOTES:

LEADERSHIP KEYS: ☐ DISCOVER ☐ CONNECT ☐ TAKE ACTION PROCESSES: ☐ GIRL-LED ☐ LEARNING BY DOING ☐ COOPERATIVE LEARNING

STEP 3:

TIME NEEDED: .... MINUTES

ACTIVITY: .... TO BE COMPLETED AT: ☐ HOME ☐ MEETING ☐ EVENT ☐ FIELD TRIP

PREP/SUPPLIES NEEDED: WHO'S RESPONSIBLE?

(1) .... ☐ LEADER ☐ GIRL/VOLUNTEER: ....

(2) .... ☐ LEADER ☐ GIRL/VOLUNTEER: ....

(3) .... ☐ LEADER ☐ GIRL/VOLUNTEER: ....

(4) .... ☐ LEADER ☐ GIRL/VOLUNTEER: ....

(5) .... ☐ LEADER ☐ GIRL/VOLUNTEER: ....

ACTIVITY STEPS/NOTES:

LEADERSHIP KEYS: ☐ DISCOVER ☐ CONNECT ☐ TAKE ACTION PROCESSES: ☐ GIRL-LED ☐ LEARNING BY DOING ☐ COOPERATIVE LEARNING

STEP 4:

TIME NEEDED: .... MINUTES

ACTIVITY: .... TO BE COMPLETED AT: ☐ HOME ☐ MEETING ☐ EVENT ☐ FIELD TRIP

PREP/SUPPLIES NEEDED: WHO'S RESPONSIBLE?

(1) .... ☐ LEADER ☐ GIRL/VOLUNTEER: ....

(2) .... ☐ LEADER ☐ GIRL/VOLUNTEER: ....

(3) .... ☐ LEADER ☐ GIRL/VOLUNTEER: ....

(4) .... ☐ LEADER ☐ GIRL/VOLUNTEER: ....

(5) .... ☐ LEADER ☐ GIRL/VOLUNTEER: ....

ACTIVITY STEPS/NOTES:

LEADERSHIP KEYS: ☐ DISCOVER ☐ CONNECT ☐ TAKE ACTION PROCESSES: ☐ GIRL-LED ☐ LEARNING BY DOING ☐ COOPERATIVE LEARNING

STEP 5:

TIME NEEDED: .... MINUTES

ACTIVITY: .... TO BE COMPLETED AT: ☐ HOME ☐ MEETING ☐ EVENT ☐ FIELD TRIP

PREP/SUPPLIES NEEDED: WHO'S RESPONSIBLE?

(1) .... ☐ LEADER ☐ GIRL/VOLUNTEER: ....

(2) .... ☐ LEADER ☐ GIRL/VOLUNTEER: ....

(3) .... ☐ LEADER ☐ GIRL/VOLUNTEER: ....

(4) .... ☐ LEADER ☐ GIRL/VOLUNTEER: ....

(5) .... ☐ LEADER ☐ GIRL/VOLUNTEER: ....

ACTIVITY STEPS/NOTES:

LEADERSHIP KEYS: ☐ DISCOVER ☐ CONNECT ☐ TAKE ACTION PROCESSES: ☐ GIRL-LED ☐ LEARNING BY DOING ☐ COOPERATIVE LEARNING

BADGE ACTIVITIES PLANNER

BADGE:

PURPOSE: ....

OF MEETINGS TO COMPLETE THIS BADGE: .... JOURNEY CONNECTION(S): .... ☐ STEP 1 ☐ STEP 2 ☐ STEP 3 ☐ STEP 4 ☐ STEP 5

LONG-TERM PLANNING:

FIELD TRIP/GUEST SPEAKER IDEAS:

STEP 1:

TIME NEEDED: .... MINUTES

ACTIVITY: .... TO BE COMPLETED AT: ☐ HOME ☐ MEETING ☐ EVENT ☐ FIELD TRIP

PREP/SUPPLIES NEEDED: WHO'S RESPONSIBLE?

(1) .... ☐ LEADER ☐ GIRL/VOLUNTEER: ....

(2) .... ☐ LEADER ☐ GIRL/VOLUNTEER: ....

(3) .... ☐ LEADER ☐ GIRL/VOLUNTEER: ....

(4) .... ☐ LEADER ☐ GIRL/VOLUNTEER: ....

(5) .... ☐ LEADER ☐ GIRL/VOLUNTEER: ....

ACTIVITY STEPS/NOTES:

LEADERSHIP KEYS: ☐ DISCOVER ☐ CONNECT ☐ TAKE ACTION PROCESSES: ☐ GIRL-LED ☐ LEARNING BY DOING ☐ COOPERATIVE LEARNING

STEP 2:

TIME NEEDED: .... MINUTES

ACTIVITY: .... TO BE COMPLETED AT: ☐ HOME ☐ MEETING ☐ EVENT ☐ FIELD TRIP

PREP/SUPPLIES NEEDED: WHO'S RESPONSIBLE?

(1) .... ☐ LEADER ☐ GIRL/VOLUNTEER: ....

(2) .... ☐ LEADER ☐ GIRL/VOLUNTEER: ....

(3) .... ☐ LEADER ☐ GIRL/VOLUNTEER: ....

(4) .... ☐ LEADER ☐ GIRL/VOLUNTEER: ....

(5) .... ☐ LEADER ☐ GIRL/VOLUNTEER: ....

ACTIVITY STEPS/NOTES:

LEADERSHIP KEYS: ☐ DISCOVER ☐ CONNECT ☐ TAKE ACTION PROCESSES: ☐ GIRL-LED ☐ LEARNING BY DOING ☐ COOPERATIVE LEARNING

STEP 3:

TIME NEEDED: .... MINUTES

ACTIVITY: .... TO BE COMPLETED AT: ☐ HOME ☐ MEETING ☐ EVENT ☐ FIELD TRIP

PREP/SUPPLIES NEEDED: WHO'S RESPONSIBLE?

(1) .... ☐ LEADER ☐ GIRL/VOLUNTEER: ....

(2) .... ☐ LEADER ☐ GIRL/VOLUNTEER: ....

(3) .... ☐ LEADER ☐ GIRL/VOLUNTEER: ....

(4) .... ☐ LEADER ☐ GIRL/VOLUNTEER: ....

(5) .... ☐ LEADER ☐ GIRL/VOLUNTEER: ....

ACTIVITY STEPS/NOTES:

LEADERSHIP KEYS: ☐ DISCOVER ☐ CONNECT ☐ TAKE ACTION PROCESSES: ☐ GIRL-LED ☐ LEARNING BY DOING ☐ COOPERATIVE LEARNING

STEP 4:

TIME NEEDED: .... MINUTES

ACTIVITY: .... TO BE COMPLETED AT: ☐ HOME ☐ MEETING ☐ EVENT ☐ FIELD TRIP

PREP/SUPPLIES NEEDED: WHO'S RESPONSIBLE?

(1) .... ☐ LEADER ☐ GIRL/VOLUNTEER: ....

(2) .... ☐ LEADER ☐ GIRL/VOLUNTEER: ....

(3) .... ☐ LEADER ☐ GIRL/VOLUNTEER: ....

(4) .... ☐ LEADER ☐ GIRL/VOLUNTEER: ....

(5) .... ☐ LEADER ☐ GIRL/VOLUNTEER: ....

ACTIVITY STEPS/NOTES:

LEADERSHIP KEYS: ☐ DISCOVER ☐ CONNECT ☐ TAKE ACTION PROCESSES: ☐ GIRL-LED ☐ LEARNING BY DOING ☐ COOPERATIVE LEARNING

STEP 5:

TIME NEEDED: .... MINUTES

ACTIVITY: .... TO BE COMPLETED AT: ☐ HOME ☐ MEETING ☐ EVENT ☐ FIELD TRIP

PREP/SUPPLIES NEEDED: WHO'S RESPONSIBLE?

(1) .... ☐ LEADER ☐ GIRL/VOLUNTEER: ....

(2) .... ☐ LEADER ☐ GIRL/VOLUNTEER: ....

(3) .... ☐ LEADER ☐ GIRL/VOLUNTEER: ....

(4) .... ☐ LEADER ☐ GIRL/VOLUNTEER: ....

(5) .... ☐ LEADER ☐ GIRL/VOLUNTEER: ....

ACTIVITY STEPS/NOTES:

LEADERSHIP KEYS: ☐ DISCOVER ☐ CONNECT ☐ TAKE ACTION PROCESSES: ☐ GIRL-LED ☐ LEARNING BY DOING ☐ COOPERATIVE LEARNING

BADGE ACTIVITIES PLANNER

BADGE:

PURPOSE: ....

OF MEETINGS TO COMPLETE THIS BADGE: .... JOURNEY CONNECTION(S): .... ☐ STEP 1 ☐ STEP 2 ☐ STEP 3 ☐ STEP 4 ☐ STEP 5

LONG-TERM PLANNING:

FIELD TRIP/GUEST SPEAKER IDEAS:

STEP 1:

TIME NEEDED: .... MINUTES

ACTIVITY: .... TO BE COMPLETED AT: ☐ HOME ☐ MEETING ☐ EVENT ☐ FIELD TRIP

PREP/SUPPLIES NEEDED:

WHO'S RESPONSIBLE?

(1) .... ☐ LEADER ☐ GIRL/VOLUNTEER: ....

(2) .... ☐ LEADER ☐ GIRL/VOLUNTEER: ....

(3) .... ☐ LEADER ☐ GIRL/VOLUNTEER: ....

(4) .... ☐ LEADER ☐ GIRL/VOLUNTEER: ....

(5) .... ☐ LEADER ☐ GIRL/VOLUNTEER: ....

ACTIVITY STEPS/NOTES:

LEADERSHIP KEYS: ☐ DISCOVER ☐ CONNECT ☐ TAKE ACTION PROCESSES: ☐ GIRL-LED ☐ LEARNING BY DOING ☐ COOPERATIVE LEARNING

STEP 2:

TIME NEEDED: .... MINUTES

ACTIVITY: .... TO BE COMPLETED AT: ☐ HOME ☐ MEETING ☐ EVENT ☐ FIELD TRIP

PREP/SUPPLIES NEEDED:

WHO'S RESPONSIBLE?

(1) .... ☐ LEADER ☐ GIRL/VOLUNTEER: ....

(2) .... ☐ LEADER ☐ GIRL/VOLUNTEER: ....

(3) .... ☐ LEADER ☐ GIRL/VOLUNTEER: ....

(4) .... ☐ LEADER ☐ GIRL/VOLUNTEER: ....

(5) .... ☐ LEADER ☐ GIRL/VOLUNTEER: ....

ACTIVITY STEPS/NOTES:

LEADERSHIP KEYS: ☐ DISCOVER ☐ CONNECT ☐ TAKE ACTION PROCESSES: ☐ GIRL-LED ☐ LEARNING BY DOING ☐ COOPERATIVE LEARNING

STEP 3:

TIME NEEDED: .... MINUTES

ACTIVITY: .... TO BE COMPLETED AT: ☐ HOME ☐ MEETING ☐ EVENT ☐ FIELD TRIP

PREP/SUPPLIES NEEDED: WHO'S RESPONSIBLE?

(1) .... ☐ LEADER ☐ GIRL/VOLUNTEER: ....

(2) .... ☐ LEADER ☐ GIRL/VOLUNTEER: ....

(3) .... ☐ LEADER ☐ GIRL/VOLUNTEER: ....

(4) .... ☐ LEADER ☐ GIRL/VOLUNTEER: ....

(5) .... ☐ LEADER ☐ GIRL/VOLUNTEER: ....

ACTIVITY STEPS/NOTES:

LEADERSHIP KEYS: ☐ DISCOVER ☐ CONNECT ☐ TAKE ACTION PROCESSES: ☐ GIRL-LED ☐ LEARNING BY DOING ☐ COOPERATIVE LEARNING

STEP 4:

TIME NEEDED: .... MINUTES

ACTIVITY: .... TO BE COMPLETED AT: ☐ HOME ☐ MEETING ☐ EVENT ☐ FIELD TRIP

PREP/SUPPLIES NEEDED: WHO'S RESPONSIBLE?

(1) .... ☐ LEADER ☐ GIRL/VOLUNTEER: ....

(2) .... ☐ LEADER ☐ GIRL/VOLUNTEER: ....

(3) .... ☐ LEADER ☐ GIRL/VOLUNTEER: ....

(4) .... ☐ LEADER ☐ GIRL/VOLUNTEER: ....

(5) .... ☐ LEADER ☐ GIRL/VOLUNTEER: ....

ACTIVITY STEPS/NOTES:

LEADERSHIP KEYS: ☐ DISCOVER ☐ CONNECT ☐ TAKE ACTION PROCESSES: ☐ GIRL-LED ☐ LEARNING BY DOING ☐ COOPERATIVE LEARNING

STEP 5:

TIME NEEDED: .... MINUTES

ACTIVITY: .... TO BE COMPLETED AT: ☐ HOME ☐ MEETING ☐ EVENT ☐ FIELD TRIP

PREP/SUPPLIES NEEDED: WHO'S RESPONSIBLE?

(1) .... ☐ LEADER ☐ GIRL/VOLUNTEER: ....

(2) .... ☐ LEADER ☐ GIRL/VOLUNTEER: ....

(3) .... ☐ LEADER ☐ GIRL/VOLUNTEER: ....

(4) .... ☐ LEADER ☐ GIRL/VOLUNTEER: ....

(5) .... ☐ LEADER ☐ GIRL/VOLUNTEER: ....

ACTIVITY STEPS/NOTES:

LEADERSHIP KEYS: ☐ DISCOVER ☐ CONNECT ☐ TAKE ACTION PROCESSES: ☐ GIRL-LED ☐ LEARNING BY DOING ☐ COOPERATIVE LEARNING

BADGE ACTIVITIES PLANNER

BADGE:

PURPOSE: ....

OF MEETINGS TO COMPLETE THIS BADGE: .... JOURNEY CONNECTION(S): .... ☐ STEP 1 ☐ STEP 2 ☐ STEP 3 ☐ STEP 4 ☐ STEP 5

LONG-TERM PLANNING:

FIELD TRIP/GUEST SPEAKER IDEAS:

STEP 1:

TIME NEEDED: .... MINUTES

ACTIVITY: .... TO BE COMPLETED AT: ☐ HOME ☐ MEETING ☐ EVENT ☐ FIELD TRIP

PREP/SUPPLIES NEEDED: WHO'S RESPONSIBLE?

(1) .... ☐ LEADER ☐ GIRL/VOLUNTEER: ....

(2) .... ☐ LEADER ☐ GIRL/VOLUNTEER: ....

(3) .... ☐ LEADER ☐ GIRL/VOLUNTEER: ....

(4) .... ☐ LEADER ☐ GIRL/VOLUNTEER: ....

(5) .... ☐ LEADER ☐ GIRL/VOLUNTEER: ....

ACTIVITY STEPS/NOTES:

LEADERSHIP KEYS: ☐ DISCOVER ☐ CONNECT ☐ TAKE ACTION PROCESSES: ☐ GIRL-LED ☐ LEARNING BY DOING ☐ COOPERATIVE LEARNING

STEP 2:

TIME NEEDED: .... MINUTES

ACTIVITY: .... TO BE COMPLETED AT: ☐ HOME ☐ MEETING ☐ EVENT ☐ FIELD TRIP

PREP/SUPPLIES NEEDED: WHO'S RESPONSIBLE?

(1) .... ☐ LEADER ☐ GIRL/VOLUNTEER: ....

(2) .... ☐ LEADER ☐ GIRL/VOLUNTEER: ....

(3) .... ☐ LEADER ☐ GIRL/VOLUNTEER: ....

(4) .... ☐ LEADER ☐ GIRL/VOLUNTEER: ....

(5) .... ☐ LEADER ☐ GIRL/VOLUNTEER: ....

ACTIVITY STEPS/NOTES:

LEADERSHIP KEYS: ☐ DISCOVER ☐ CONNECT ☐ TAKE ACTION PROCESSES: ☐ GIRL-LED ☐ LEARNING BY DOING ☐ COOPERATIVE LEARNING

STEP 3:

TIME NEEDED: .... MINUTES

ACTIVITY: .... TO BE COMPLETED AT: ☐ HOME ☐ MEETING ☐ EVENT ☐ FIELD TRIP

PREP/SUPPLIES NEEDED: WHO'S RESPONSIBLE?

(1) .... ☐ LEADER ☐ GIRL/VOLUNTEER: ....

(2) .... ☐ LEADER ☐ GIRL/VOLUNTEER: ....

(3) .... ☐ LEADER ☐ GIRL/VOLUNTEER: ....

(4) .... ☐ LEADER ☐ GIRL/VOLUNTEER: ....

(5) .... ☐ LEADER ☐ GIRL/VOLUNTEER: ....

ACTIVITY STEPS/NOTES:

LEADERSHIP KEYS: ☐ DISCOVER ☐ CONNECT ☐ TAKE ACTION PROCESSES: ☐ GIRL-LED ☐ LEARNING BY DOING ☐ COOPERATIVE LEARNING

STEP 4:

TIME NEEDED: .... MINUTES

ACTIVITY: .... TO BE COMPLETED AT: ☐ HOME ☐ MEETING ☐ EVENT ☐ FIELD TRIP

PREP/SUPPLIES NEEDED: WHO'S RESPONSIBLE?

(1) .... ☐ LEADER ☐ GIRL/VOLUNTEER: ....

(2) .... ☐ LEADER ☐ GIRL/VOLUNTEER: ....

(3) .... ☐ LEADER ☐ GIRL/VOLUNTEER: ....

(4) .... ☐ LEADER ☐ GIRL/VOLUNTEER: ....

(5) .... ☐ LEADER ☐ GIRL/VOLUNTEER: ....

ACTIVITY STEPS/NOTES:

LEADERSHIP KEYS: ☐ DISCOVER ☐ CONNECT ☐ TAKE ACTION PROCESSES: ☐ GIRL-LED ☐ LEARNING BY DOING ☐ COOPERATIVE LEARNING

STEP 5:

TIME NEEDED: .... MINUTES

ACTIVITY: .... TO BE COMPLETED AT: ☐ HOME ☐ MEETING ☐ EVENT ☐ FIELD TRIP

PREP/SUPPLIES NEEDED: WHO'S RESPONSIBLE?

(1) .... ☐ LEADER ☐ GIRL/VOLUNTEER: ....

(2) .... ☐ LEADER ☐ GIRL/VOLUNTEER: ....

(3) .... ☐ LEADER ☐ GIRL/VOLUNTEER: ....

(4) .... ☐ LEADER ☐ GIRL/VOLUNTEER: ....

(5) .... ☐ LEADER ☐ GIRL/VOLUNTEER: ....

ACTIVITY STEPS/NOTES:

LEADERSHIP KEYS: ☐ DISCOVER ☐ CONNECT ☐ TAKE ACTION PROCESSES: ☐ GIRL-LED ☐ LEARNING BY DOING ☐ COOPERATIVE LEARNING

BADGE ACTIVITIES PLANNER

BADGE:

PURPOSE: ....

OF MEETINGS TO COMPLETE THIS BADGE: .... JOURNEY CONNECTION(S): .... ☐ STEP 1 ☐ STEP 2 ☐ STEP 3 ☐ STEP 4 ☐ STEP 5

LONG-TERM PLANNING:

FIELD TRIP/GUEST SPEAKER IDEAS:

STEP 1:

TIME NEEDED: .... MINUTES

ACTIVITY: .... TO BE COMPLETED AT: ☐ HOME ☐ MEETING ☐ EVENT ☐ FIELD TRIP

PREP/SUPPLIES NEEDED: WHO'S RESPONSIBLE?

(1) .... ☐ LEADER ☐ GIRL/VOLUNTEER: ....

(2) .... ☐ LEADER ☐ GIRL/VOLUNTEER: ....

(3) .... ☐ LEADER ☐ GIRL/VOLUNTEER: ....

(4) .... ☐ LEADER ☐ GIRL/VOLUNTEER: ....

(5) .... ☐ LEADER ☐ GIRL/VOLUNTEER: ....

ACTIVITY STEPS/NOTES:

LEADERSHIP KEYS: ☐ DISCOVER ☐ CONNECT ☐ TAKE ACTION PROCESSES: ☐ GIRL-LED ☐ LEARNING BY DOING ☐ COOPERATIVE LEARNING

STEP 2:

TIME NEEDED: .... MINUTES

ACTIVITY: .... TO BE COMPLETED AT: ☐ HOME ☐ MEETING ☐ EVENT ☐ FIELD TRIP

PREP/SUPPLIES NEEDED: WHO'S RESPONSIBLE?

(1) .... ☐ LEADER ☐ GIRL/VOLUNTEER: ....

(2) .... ☐ LEADER ☐ GIRL/VOLUNTEER: ....

(3) .... ☐ LEADER ☐ GIRL/VOLUNTEER: ....

(4) .... ☐ LEADER ☐ GIRL/VOLUNTEER: ....

(5) .... ☐ LEADER ☐ GIRL/VOLUNTEER: ....

ACTIVITY STEPS/NOTES:

LEADERSHIP KEYS: ☐ DISCOVER ☐ CONNECT ☐ TAKE ACTION PROCESSES: ☐ GIRL-LED ☐ LEARNING BY DOING ☐ COOPERATIVE LEARNING

STEP 3:

TIME NEEDED: .... MINUTES

ACTIVITY: .... TO BE COMPLETED AT: ☐ HOME ☐ MEETING ☐ EVENT ☐ FIELD TRIP

PREP/SUPPLIES NEEDED: WHO'S RESPONSIBLE?

(1) .... ☐ LEADER ☐ GIRL/VOLUNTEER: ....

(2) .... ☐ LEADER ☐ GIRL/VOLUNTEER: ....

(3) .... ☐ LEADER ☐ GIRL/VOLUNTEER: ....

(4) .... ☐ LEADER ☐ GIRL/VOLUNTEER: ....

(5) .... ☐ LEADER ☐ GIRL/VOLUNTEER: ....

ACTIVITY STEPS/NOTES:

LEADERSHIP KEYS: ☐ DISCOVER ☐ CONNECT ☐ TAKE ACTION PROCESSES: ☐ GIRL-LED ☐ LEARNING BY DOING ☐ COOPERATIVE LEARNING

STEP 4:

TIME NEEDED: .... MINUTES

ACTIVITY: .... TO BE COMPLETED AT: ☐ HOME ☐ MEETING ☐ EVENT ☐ FIELD TRIP

PREP/SUPPLIES NEEDED: WHO'S RESPONSIBLE?

(1) .... ☐ LEADER ☐ GIRL/VOLUNTEER: ....

(2) .... ☐ LEADER ☐ GIRL/VOLUNTEER: ....

(3) .... ☐ LEADER ☐ GIRL/VOLUNTEER: ....

(4) .... ☐ LEADER ☐ GIRL/VOLUNTEER: ....

(5) .... ☐ LEADER ☐ GIRL/VOLUNTEER: ....

ACTIVITY STEPS/NOTES:

LEADERSHIP KEYS: ☐ DISCOVER ☐ CONNECT ☐ TAKE ACTION PROCESSES: ☐ GIRL-LED ☐ LEARNING BY DOING ☐ COOPERATIVE LEARNING

STEP 5:

TIME NEEDED: .... MINUTES

ACTIVITY: .... TO BE COMPLETED AT: ☐ HOME ☐ MEETING ☐ EVENT ☐ FIELD TRIP

PREP/SUPPLIES NEEDED: WHO'S RESPONSIBLE?

(1) .... ☐ LEADER ☐ GIRL/VOLUNTEER: ....

(2) .... ☐ LEADER ☐ GIRL/VOLUNTEER: ....

(3) .... ☐ LEADER ☐ GIRL/VOLUNTEER: ....

(4) .... ☐ LEADER ☐ GIRL/VOLUNTEER: ....

(5) .... ☐ LEADER ☐ GIRL/VOLUNTEER: ....

ACTIVITY STEPS/NOTES:

LEADERSHIP KEYS: ☐ DISCOVER ☐ CONNECT ☐ TAKE ACTION PROCESSES: ☐ GIRL-LED ☐ LEARNING BY DOING ☐ COOPERATIVE LEARNING

BADGE ACTIVITIES PLANNER

BADGE:

PURPOSE: ....

OF MEETINGS TO COMPLETE THIS BADGE: .... JOURNEY CONNECTION(S): .... ☐ STEP 1 ☐ STEP 2 ☐ STEP 3 ☐ STEP 4 ☐ STEP 5

LONG-TERM PLANNING:

FIELD TRIP/GUEST SPEAKER IDEAS:

STEP 1:

TIME NEEDED: .... MINUTES

ACTIVITY: .... TO BE COMPLETED AT: ☐ HOME ☐ MEETING ☐ EVENT ☐ FIELD TRIP

PREP/SUPPLIES NEEDED: — WHO'S RESPONSIBLE?

(1) .... ☐ LEADER ☐ GIRL/VOLUNTEER: ....

(2) .... ☐ LEADER ☐ GIRL/VOLUNTEER: ....

(3) .... ☐ LEADER ☐ GIRL/VOLUNTEER: ....

(4) .... ☐ LEADER ☐ GIRL/VOLUNTEER: ....

(5) .... ☐ LEADER ☐ GIRL/VOLUNTEER: ....

ACTIVITY STEPS/NOTES:

LEADERSHIP KEYS: ☐ DISCOVER ☐ CONNECT ☐ TAKE ACTION PROCESSES: ☐ GIRL-LED ☐ LEARNING BY DOING ☐ COOPERATIVE LEARNING

STEP 2:

TIME NEEDED: .... MINUTES

ACTIVITY: .... TO BE COMPLETED AT: ☐ HOME ☐ MEETING ☐ EVENT ☐ FIELD TRIP

PREP/SUPPLIES NEEDED: — WHO'S RESPONSIBLE?

(1) .... ☐ LEADER ☐ GIRL/VOLUNTEER: ....

(2) .... ☐ LEADER ☐ GIRL/VOLUNTEER: ....

(3) .... ☐ LEADER ☐ GIRL/VOLUNTEER: ....

(4) .... ☐ LEADER ☐ GIRL/VOLUNTEER: ....

(5) .... ☐ LEADER ☐ GIRL/VOLUNTEER: ....

ACTIVITY STEPS/NOTES:

LEADERSHIP KEYS: ☐ DISCOVER ☐ CONNECT ☐ TAKE ACTION PROCESSES: ☐ GIRL-LED ☐ LEARNING BY DOING ☐ COOPERATIVE LEARNING

STEP 3:

TIME NEEDED: .... MINUTES

ACTIVITY: .... TO BE COMPLETED AT: ☐ HOME ☐ MEETING ☐ EVENT ☐ FIELD TRIP

PREP/SUPPLIES NEEDED: WHO'S RESPONSIBLE?

(1) .... ☐ LEADER ☐ GIRL/VOLUNTEER: ....

(2) .... ☐ LEADER ☐ GIRL/VOLUNTEER: ....

(3) .... ☐ LEADER ☐ GIRL/VOLUNTEER: ....

(4) .... ☐ LEADER ☐ GIRL/VOLUNTEER: ....

(5) .... ☐ LEADER ☐ GIRL/VOLUNTEER: ....

ACTIVITY STEPS/NOTES:

LEADERSHIP KEYS: ☐ DISCOVER ☐ CONNECT ☐ TAKE ACTION PROCESSES: ☐ GIRL-LED ☐ LEARNING BY DOING ☐ COOPERATIVE LEARNING

STEP 4:

TIME NEEDED: .... MINUTES

ACTIVITY: .... TO BE COMPLETED AT: ☐ HOME ☐ MEETING ☐ EVENT ☐ FIELD TRIP

PREP/SUPPLIES NEEDED: WHO'S RESPONSIBLE?

(1) .... ☐ LEADER ☐ GIRL/VOLUNTEER: ....

(2) .... ☐ LEADER ☐ GIRL/VOLUNTEER: ....

(3) .... ☐ LEADER ☐ GIRL/VOLUNTEER: ....

(4) .... ☐ LEADER ☐ GIRL/VOLUNTEER: ....

(5) .... ☐ LEADER ☐ GIRL/VOLUNTEER: ....

ACTIVITY STEPS/NOTES:

LEADERSHIP KEYS: ☐ DISCOVER ☐ CONNECT ☐ TAKE ACTION PROCESSES: ☐ GIRL-LED ☐ LEARNING BY DOING ☐ COOPERATIVE LEARNING

STEP 5:

TIME NEEDED: .... MINUTES

ACTIVITY: .... TO BE COMPLETED AT: ☐ HOME ☐ MEETING ☐ EVENT ☐ FIELD TRIP

PREP/SUPPLIES NEEDED: WHO'S RESPONSIBLE?

(1) .... ☐ LEADER ☐ GIRL/VOLUNTEER: ....

(2) .... ☐ LEADER ☐ GIRL/VOLUNTEER: ....

(3) .... ☐ LEADER ☐ GIRL/VOLUNTEER: ....

(4) .... ☐ LEADER ☐ GIRL/VOLUNTEER: ....

(5) .... ☐ LEADER ☐ GIRL/VOLUNTEER: ....

ACTIVITY STEPS/NOTES:

LEADERSHIP KEYS: ☐ DISCOVER ☐ CONNECT ☐ TAKE ACTION PROCESSES: ☐ GIRL-LED ☐ LEARNING BY DOING ☐ COOPERATIVE LEARNING

BADGE ACTIVITIES PLANNER

BADGE:

PURPOSE: ....

OF MEETINGS TO COMPLETE THIS BADGE: .... JOURNEY CONNECTION(S): .... ☐ STEP 1 ☐ STEP 2 ☐ STEP 3 ☐ STEP 4 ☐ STEP 5

LONG-TERM PLANNING:

FIELD TRIP/GUEST SPEAKER IDEAS:

STEP 1:

TIME NEEDED: .... MINUTES

ACTIVITY: .... TO BE COMPLETED AT: ☐ HOME ☐ MEETING ☐ EVENT ☐ FIELD TRIP

PREP/SUPPLIES NEEDED:

WHO'S RESPONSIBLE?

(1) .... ☐ LEADER ☐ GIRL/VOLUNTEER: ....

(2) .... ☐ LEADER ☐ GIRL/VOLUNTEER: ....

(3) .... ☐ LEADER ☐ GIRL/VOLUNTEER: ....

(4) .... ☐ LEADER ☐ GIRL/VOLUNTEER: ....

(5) .... ☐ LEADER ☐ GIRL/VOLUNTEER: ....

ACTIVITY STEPS/NOTES:

LEADERSHIP KEYS: ☐ DISCOVER ☐ CONNECT ☐ TAKE ACTION PROCESSES: ☐ GIRL-LED ☐ LEARNING BY DOING ☐ COOPERATIVE LEARNING

STEP 2:

TIME NEEDED: .... MINUTES

ACTIVITY: .... TO BE COMPLETED AT: ☐ HOME ☐ MEETING ☐ EVENT ☐ FIELD TRIP

PREP/SUPPLIES NEEDED:

WHO'S RESPONSIBLE?

(1) .... ☐ LEADER ☐ GIRL/VOLUNTEER: ....

(2) .... ☐ LEADER ☐ GIRL/VOLUNTEER: ....

(3) .... ☐ LEADER ☐ GIRL/VOLUNTEER: ....

(4) .... ☐ LEADER ☐ GIRL/VOLUNTEER: ....

(5) .... ☐ LEADER ☐ GIRL/VOLUNTEER: ....

ACTIVITY STEPS/NOTES:

LEADERSHIP KEYS: ☐ DISCOVER ☐ CONNECT ☐ TAKE ACTION PROCESSES: ☐ GIRL-LED ☐ LEARNING BY DOING ☐ COOPERATIVE LEARNING

STEP 3:

TIME NEEDED: .... MINUTES

ACTIVITY: .... TO BE COMPLETED AT: ☐ HOME ☐ MEETING ☐ EVENT ☐ FIELD TRIP

PREP/SUPPLIES NEEDED: WHO'S RESPONSIBLE?

(1) .... ☐ LEADER ☐ GIRL/VOLUNTEER: ....

(2) .... ☐ LEADER ☐ GIRL/VOLUNTEER: ....

(3) .... ☐ LEADER ☐ GIRL/VOLUNTEER: ....

(4) .... ☐ LEADER ☐ GIRL/VOLUNTEER: ....

(5) .... ☐ LEADER ☐ GIRL/VOLUNTEER: ....

ACTIVITY STEPS/NOTES:

LEADERSHIP KEYS: ☐ DISCOVER ☐ CONNECT ☐ TAKE ACTION PROCESSES: ☐ GIRL-LED ☐ LEARNING BY DOING ☐ COOPERATIVE LEARNING

STEP 4:

TIME NEEDED: .... MINUTES

ACTIVITY: .... TO BE COMPLETED AT: ☐ HOME ☐ MEETING ☐ EVENT ☐ FIELD TRIP

PREP/SUPPLIES NEEDED: WHO'S RESPONSIBLE?

(1) .... ☐ LEADER ☐ GIRL/VOLUNTEER: ....

(2) .... ☐ LEADER ☐ GIRL/VOLUNTEER: ....

(3) .... ☐ LEADER ☐ GIRL/VOLUNTEER: ....

(4) .... ☐ LEADER ☐ GIRL/VOLUNTEER: ....

(5) .... ☐ LEADER ☐ GIRL/VOLUNTEER: ....

ACTIVITY STEPS/NOTES:

LEADERSHIP KEYS: ☐ DISCOVER ☐ CONNECT ☐ TAKE ACTION PROCESSES: ☐ GIRL-LED ☐ LEARNING BY DOING ☐ COOPERATIVE LEARNING

STEP 5:

TIME NEEDED: .... MINUTES

ACTIVITY: .... TO BE COMPLETED AT: ☐ HOME ☐ MEETING ☐ EVENT ☐ FIELD TRIP

PREP/SUPPLIES NEEDED: WHO'S RESPONSIBLE?

(1) .... ☐ LEADER ☐ GIRL/VOLUNTEER: ....

(2) .... ☐ LEADER ☐ GIRL/VOLUNTEER: ....

(3) .... ☐ LEADER ☐ GIRL/VOLUNTEER: ....

(4) .... ☐ LEADER ☐ GIRL/VOLUNTEER: ....

(5) .... ☐ LEADER ☐ GIRL/VOLUNTEER: ....

ACTIVITY STEPS/NOTES:

LEADERSHIP KEYS: ☐ DISCOVER ☐ CONNECT ☐ TAKE ACTION PROCESSES: ☐ GIRL-LED ☐ LEARNING BY DOING ☐ COOPERATIVE LEARNING

BADGE ACTIVITIES PLANNER

BADGE:

PURPOSE: ....

OF MEETINGS TO COMPLETE THIS BADGE: .... JOURNEY CONNECTION(S): .... ☐ STEP 1 ☐ STEP 2 ☐ STEP 3 ☐ STEP 4 ☐ STEP 5

LONG-TERM PLANNING:

FIELD TRIP/GUEST SPEAKER IDEAS:

STEP 1:

TIME NEEDED: .... MINUTES

ACTIVITY: .... TO BE COMPLETED AT: ☐ HOME ☐ MEETING ☐ EVENT ☐ FIELD TRIP

PREP/SUPPLIES NEEDED: WHO'S RESPONSIBLE?

(1) .... ☐ LEADER ☐ GIRL/VOLUNTEER: ....

(2) .... ☐ LEADER ☐ GIRL/VOLUNTEER: ....

(3) .... ☐ LEADER ☐ GIRL/VOLUNTEER: ....

(4) .... ☐ LEADER ☐ GIRL/VOLUNTEER: ....

(5) .... ☐ LEADER ☐ GIRL/VOLUNTEER: ....

ACTIVITY STEPS/NOTES:

LEADERSHIP KEYS: ☐ DISCOVER ☐ CONNECT ☐ TAKE ACTION PROCESSES: ☐ GIRL-LED ☐ LEARNING BY DOING ☐ COOPERATIVE LEARNING

STEP 2:

TIME NEEDED: .... MINUTES

ACTIVITY: .... TO BE COMPLETED AT: ☐ HOME ☐ MEETING ☐ EVENT ☐ FIELD TRIP

PREP/SUPPLIES NEEDED: WHO'S RESPONSIBLE?

(1) .... ☐ LEADER ☐ GIRL/VOLUNTEER: ....

(2) .... ☐ LEADER ☐ GIRL/VOLUNTEER: ....

(3) .... ☐ LEADER ☐ GIRL/VOLUNTEER: ....

(4) .... ☐ LEADER ☐ GIRL/VOLUNTEER: ....

(5) .... ☐ LEADER ☐ GIRL/VOLUNTEER: ....

ACTIVITY STEPS/NOTES:

LEADERSHIP KEYS: ☐ DISCOVER ☐ CONNECT ☐ TAKE ACTION PROCESSES: ☐ GIRL-LED ☐ LEARNING BY DOING ☐ COOPERATIVE LEARNING

STEP 3:

TIME NEEDED: .... MINUTES

ACTIVITY: .... TO BE COMPLETED AT: ☐ HOME ☐ MEETING ☐ EVENT ☐ FIELD TRIP

PREP/SUPPLIES NEEDED: WHO'S RESPONSIBLE?

(1) .... ☐ LEADER ☐ GIRL/VOLUNTEER: ....

(2) .... ☐ LEADER ☐ GIRL/VOLUNTEER: ....

(3) .... ☐ LEADER ☐ GIRL/VOLUNTEER: ....

(4) .... ☐ LEADER ☐ GIRL/VOLUNTEER: ....

(5) .... ☐ LEADER ☐ GIRL/VOLUNTEER: ....

ACTIVITY STEPS/NOTES:

LEADERSHIP KEYS: ☐ DISCOVER ☐ CONNECT ☐ TAKE ACTION PROCESSES: ☐ GIRL-LED ☐ LEARNING BY DOING ☐ COOPERATIVE LEARNING

STEP 4:

TIME NEEDED: .... MINUTES

ACTIVITY: .... TO BE COMPLETED AT: ☐ HOME ☐ MEETING ☐ EVENT ☐ FIELD TRIP

PREP/SUPPLIES NEEDED: WHO'S RESPONSIBLE?

(1) .... ☐ LEADER ☐ GIRL/VOLUNTEER: ....

(2) .... ☐ LEADER ☐ GIRL/VOLUNTEER: ....

(3) .... ☐ LEADER ☐ GIRL/VOLUNTEER: ....

(4) .... ☐ LEADER ☐ GIRL/VOLUNTEER: ....

(5) .... ☐ LEADER ☐ GIRL/VOLUNTEER: ....

ACTIVITY STEPS/NOTES:

LEADERSHIP KEYS: ☐ DISCOVER ☐ CONNECT ☐ TAKE ACTION PROCESSES: ☐ GIRL-LED ☐ LEARNING BY DOING ☐ COOPERATIVE LEARNING

STEP 5:

TIME NEEDED: .... MINUTES

ACTIVITY: .... TO BE COMPLETED AT: ☐ HOME ☐ MEETING ☐ EVENT ☐ FIELD TRIP

PREP/SUPPLIES NEEDED: WHO'S RESPONSIBLE?

(1) .... ☐ LEADER ☐ GIRL/VOLUNTEER: ....

(2) .... ☐ LEADER ☐ GIRL/VOLUNTEER: ....

(3) .... ☐ LEADER ☐ GIRL/VOLUNTEER: ....

(4) .... ☐ LEADER ☐ GIRL/VOLUNTEER: ....

(5) .... ☐ LEADER ☐ GIRL/VOLUNTEER: ....

ACTIVITY STEPS/NOTES:

LEADERSHIP KEYS: ☐ DISCOVER ☐ CONNECT ☐ TAKE ACTION PROCESSES: ☐ GIRL-LED ☐ LEARNING BY DOING ☐ COOPERATIVE LEARNING

BADGE ACTIVITIES PLANNER

BADGE:

PURPOSE: ....

OF MEETINGS TO COMPLETE THIS BADGE: .... JOURNEY CONNECTION(S): .... ☐ STEP 1 ☐ STEP 2 ☐ STEP 3 ☐ STEP 4 ☐ STEP 5

LONG-TERM PLANNING:

FIELD TRIP/GUEST SPEAKER IDEAS:

STEP 1:

TIME NEEDED: .... MINUTES

ACTIVITY: .... TO BE COMPLETED AT: ☐ HOME ☐ MEETING ☐ EVENT ☐ FIELD TRIP

PREP/SUPPLIES NEEDED: WHO'S RESPONSIBLE?

(1) .... ☐ LEADER ☐ GIRL/VOLUNTEER: ....

(2) .... ☐ LEADER ☐ GIRL/VOLUNTEER: ....

(3) .... ☐ LEADER ☐ GIRL/VOLUNTEER: ....

(4) .... ☐ LEADER ☐ GIRL/VOLUNTEER: ....

(5) .... ☐ LEADER ☐ GIRL/VOLUNTEER: ....

ACTIVITY STEPS/NOTES:

LEADERSHIP KEYS: ☐ DISCOVER ☐ CONNECT ☐ TAKE ACTION PROCESSES: ☐ GIRL-LED ☐ LEARNING BY DOING ☐ COOPERATIVE LEARNING

STEP 2:

TIME NEEDED: .... MINUTES

ACTIVITY: .... TO BE COMPLETED AT: ☐ HOME ☐ MEETING ☐ EVENT ☐ FIELD TRIP

PREP/SUPPLIES NEEDED: WHO'S RESPONSIBLE?

(1) .... ☐ LEADER ☐ GIRL/VOLUNTEER: ....

(2) .... ☐ LEADER ☐ GIRL/VOLUNTEER: ....

(3) .... ☐ LEADER ☐ GIRL/VOLUNTEER: ....

(4) .... ☐ LEADER ☐ GIRL/VOLUNTEER: ....

(5) .... ☐ LEADER ☐ GIRL/VOLUNTEER: ....

ACTIVITY STEPS/NOTES:

LEADERSHIP KEYS: ☐ DISCOVER ☐ CONNECT ☐ TAKE ACTION PROCESSES: ☐ GIRL-LED ☐ LEARNING BY DOING ☐ COOPERATIVE LEARNING

STEP 3:

TIME NEEDED: .... MINUTES

ACTIVITY: .... TO BE COMPLETED AT: ☐ HOME ☐ MEETING ☐ EVENT ☐ FIELD TRIP

PREP/SUPPLIES NEEDED: WHO'S RESPONSIBLE?

(1) .... ☐ LEADER ☐ GIRL/VOLUNTEER: ....

(2) .... ☐ LEADER ☐ GIRL/VOLUNTEER: ....

(3) .... ☐ LEADER ☐ GIRL/VOLUNTEER: ....

(4) .... ☐ LEADER ☐ GIRL/VOLUNTEER: ....

(5) .... ☐ LEADER ☐ GIRL/VOLUNTEER: ....

ACTIVITY STEPS/NOTES:

LEADERSHIP KEYS: ☐ DISCOVER ☐ CONNECT ☐ TAKE ACTION PROCESSES: ☐ GIRL-LED ☐ LEARNING BY DOING ☐ COOPERATIVE LEARNING

STEP 4:

TIME NEEDED: .... MINUTES

ACTIVITY: .... TO BE COMPLETED AT: ☐ HOME ☐ MEETING ☐ EVENT ☐ FIELD TRIP

PREP/SUPPLIES NEEDED: WHO'S RESPONSIBLE?

(1) .... ☐ LEADER ☐ GIRL/VOLUNTEER: ....

(2) .... ☐ LEADER ☐ GIRL/VOLUNTEER: ....

(3) .... ☐ LEADER ☐ GIRL/VOLUNTEER: ....

(4) .... ☐ LEADER ☐ GIRL/VOLUNTEER: ....

(5) .... ☐ LEADER ☐ GIRL/VOLUNTEER: ....

ACTIVITY STEPS/NOTES:

LEADERSHIP KEYS: ☐ DISCOVER ☐ CONNECT ☐ TAKE ACTION PROCESSES: ☐ GIRL-LED ☐ LEARNING BY DOING ☐ COOPERATIVE LEARNING

STEP 5:

TIME NEEDED: .... MINUTES

ACTIVITY: .... TO BE COMPLETED AT: ☐ HOME ☐ MEETING ☐ EVENT ☐ FIELD TRIP

PREP/SUPPLIES NEEDED: WHO'S RESPONSIBLE?

(1) .... ☐ LEADER ☐ GIRL/VOLUNTEER: ....

(2) .... ☐ LEADER ☐ GIRL/VOLUNTEER: ....

(3) .... ☐ LEADER ☐ GIRL/VOLUNTEER: ....

(4) .... ☐ LEADER ☐ GIRL/VOLUNTEER: ....

(5) .... ☐ LEADER ☐ GIRL/VOLUNTEER: ....

ACTIVITY STEPS/NOTES:

LEADERSHIP KEYS: ☐ DISCOVER ☐ CONNECT ☐ TAKE ACTION PROCESSES: ☐ GIRL-LED ☐ LEARNING BY DOING ☐ COOPERATIVE LEARNING

BADGE ACTIVITIES PLANNER

BADGE:

PURPOSE: ....

OF MEETINGS TO COMPLETE THIS BADGE: .... JOURNEY CONNECTION(S): .... ☐ STEP 1 ☐ STEP 2 ☐ STEP 3 ☐ STEP 4 ☐ STEP 5

LONG-TERM PLANNING:

FIELD TRIP/GUEST SPEAKER IDEAS:

STEP 1:

TIME NEEDED: .... MINUTES

ACTIVITY: .... TO BE COMPLETED AT: ☐ HOME ☐ MEETING ☐ EVENT ☐ FIELD TRIP

PREP/SUPPLIES NEEDED: WHO'S RESPONSIBLE?

(1) .... ☐ LEADER ☐ GIRL/VOLUNTEER: ....

(2) .... ☐ LEADER ☐ GIRL/VOLUNTEER: ....

(3) .... ☐ LEADER ☐ GIRL/VOLUNTEER: ....

(4) .... ☐ LEADER ☐ GIRL/VOLUNTEER: ....

(5) .... ☐ LEADER ☐ GIRL/VOLUNTEER: ....

ACTIVITY STEPS/NOTES:

LEADERSHIP KEYS: ☐ DISCOVER ☐ CONNECT ☐ TAKE ACTION PROCESSES: ☐ GIRL-LED ☐ LEARNING BY DOING ☐ COOPERATIVE LEARNING

STEP 2:

TIME NEEDED: .... MINUTES

ACTIVITY: .... TO BE COMPLETED AT: ☐ HOME ☐ MEETING ☐ EVENT ☐ FIELD TRIP

PREP/SUPPLIES NEEDED: WHO'S RESPONSIBLE?

(1) .... ☐ LEADER ☐ GIRL/VOLUNTEER: ....

(2) .... ☐ LEADER ☐ GIRL/VOLUNTEER: ....

(3) .... ☐ LEADER ☐ GIRL/VOLUNTEER: ....

(4) .... ☐ LEADER ☐ GIRL/VOLUNTEER: ....

(5) .... ☐ LEADER ☐ GIRL/VOLUNTEER: ....

ACTIVITY STEPS/NOTES:

LEADERSHIP KEYS: ☐ DISCOVER ☐ CONNECT ☐ TAKE ACTION PROCESSES: ☐ GIRL-LED ☐ LEARNING BY DOING ☐ COOPERATIVE LEARNING

STEP 3:

TIME NEEDED: .... MINUTES

ACTIVITY: .... TO BE COMPLETED AT: ☐ HOME ☐ MEETING ☐ EVENT ☐ FIELD TRIP

PREP/SUPPLIES NEEDED: WHO'S RESPONSIBLE?

(1) .... ☐ LEADER ☐ GIRL/VOLUNTEER: ....

(2) .... ☐ LEADER ☐ GIRL/VOLUNTEER: ....

(3) .... ☐ LEADER ☐ GIRL/VOLUNTEER: ....

(4) .... ☐ LEADER ☐ GIRL/VOLUNTEER: ....

(5) .... ☐ LEADER ☐ GIRL/VOLUNTEER: ....

ACTIVITY STEPS/NOTES:

LEADERSHIP KEYS: ☐ DISCOVER ☐ CONNECT ☐ TAKE ACTION PROCESSES: ☐ GIRL-LED ☐ LEARNING BY DOING ☐ COOPERATIVE LEARNING

STEP 4:

TIME NEEDED: .... MINUTES

ACTIVITY: .... TO BE COMPLETED AT: ☐ HOME ☐ MEETING ☐ EVENT ☐ FIELD TRIP

PREP/SUPPLIES NEEDED: WHO'S RESPONSIBLE?

(1) .... ☐ LEADER ☐ GIRL/VOLUNTEER: ....

(2) .... ☐ LEADER ☐ GIRL/VOLUNTEER: ....

(3) .... ☐ LEADER ☐ GIRL/VOLUNTEER: ....

(4) .... ☐ LEADER ☐ GIRL/VOLUNTEER: ....

(5) .... ☐ LEADER ☐ GIRL/VOLUNTEER: ....

ACTIVITY STEPS/NOTES:

LEADERSHIP KEYS: ☐ DISCOVER ☐ CONNECT ☐ TAKE ACTION PROCESSES: ☐ GIRL-LED ☐ LEARNING BY DOING ☐ COOPERATIVE LEARNING

STEP 5:

TIME NEEDED: .... MINUTES

ACTIVITY: .... TO BE COMPLETED AT: ☐ HOME ☐ MEETING ☐ EVENT ☐ FIELD TRIP

PREP/SUPPLIES NEEDED: WHO'S RESPONSIBLE?

(1) .... ☐ LEADER ☐ GIRL/VOLUNTEER: ....

(2) .... ☐ LEADER ☐ GIRL/VOLUNTEER: ....

(3) .... ☐ LEADER ☐ GIRL/VOLUNTEER: ....

(4) .... ☐ LEADER ☐ GIRL/VOLUNTEER: ....

(5) .... ☐ LEADER ☐ GIRL/VOLUNTEER: ....

ACTIVITY STEPS/NOTES:

LEADERSHIP KEYS: ☐ DISCOVER ☐ CONNECT ☐ TAKE ACTION PROCESSES: ☐ GIRL-LED ☐ LEARNING BY DOING ☐ COOPERATIVE LEARNING

BADGE ACTIVITIES PLANNER

BADGE:

PURPOSE: ....

OF MEETINGS TO COMPLETE THIS BADGE: .... JOURNEY CONNECTION(S): .... ☐ STEP 1 ☐ STEP 2 ☐ STEP 3 ☐ STEP 4 ☐ STEP 5

LONG-TERM PLANNING:

FIELD TRIP/GUEST SPEAKER IDEAS:

STEP 1:

TIME NEEDED: .... MINUTES

ACTIVITY: .... TO BE COMPLETED AT: ☐ HOME ☐ MEETING ☐ EVENT ☐ FIELD TRIP

PREP/SUPPLIES NEEDED: WHO'S RESPONSIBLE?

(1) .... ☐ LEADER ☐ GIRL/VOLUNTEER: ....

(2) .... ☐ LEADER ☐ GIRL/VOLUNTEER: ....

(3) .... ☐ LEADER ☐ GIRL/VOLUNTEER: ....

(4) .... ☐ LEADER ☐ GIRL/VOLUNTEER: ....

(5) .... ☐ LEADER ☐ GIRL/VOLUNTEER: ....

ACTIVITY STEPS/NOTES:

LEADERSHIP KEYS: ☐ DISCOVER ☐ CONNECT ☐ TAKE ACTION PROCESSES: ☐ GIRL-LED ☐ LEARNING BY DOING ☐ COOPERATIVE LEARNING

STEP 2:

TIME NEEDED: .... MINUTES

ACTIVITY: .... TO BE COMPLETED AT: ☐ HOME ☐ MEETING ☐ EVENT ☐ FIELD TRIP

PREP/SUPPLIES NEEDED: WHO'S RESPONSIBLE?

(1) .... ☐ LEADER ☐ GIRL/VOLUNTEER: ....

(2) .... ☐ LEADER ☐ GIRL/VOLUNTEER: ....

(3) .... ☐ LEADER ☐ GIRL/VOLUNTEER: ....

(4) .... ☐ LEADER ☐ GIRL/VOLUNTEER: ....

(5) .... ☐ LEADER ☐ GIRL/VOLUNTEER: ....

ACTIVITY STEPS/NOTES:

LEADERSHIP KEYS: ☐ DISCOVER ☐ CONNECT ☐ TAKE ACTION PROCESSES: ☐ GIRL-LED ☐ LEARNING BY DOING ☐ COOPERATIVE LEARNING

STEP 3:

TIME NEEDED: .... MINUTES

ACTIVITY: .... TO BE COMPLETED AT: ☐ HOME ☐ MEETING ☐ EVENT ☐ FIELD TRIP

PREP/SUPPLIES NEEDED: WHO'S RESPONSIBLE?

(1) .... ☐ LEADER ☐ GIRL/VOLUNTEER: ....

(2) .... ☐ LEADER ☐ GIRL/VOLUNTEER: ....

(3) .... ☐ LEADER ☐ GIRL/VOLUNTEER: ....

(4) .... ☐ LEADER ☐ GIRL/VOLUNTEER: ....

(5) .... ☐ LEADER ☐ GIRL/VOLUNTEER: ....

ACTIVITY STEPS/NOTES:

LEADERSHIP KEYS: ☐ DISCOVER ☐ CONNECT ☐ TAKE ACTION PROCESSES: ☐ GIRL-LED ☐ LEARNING BY DOING ☐ COOPERATIVE LEARNING

STEP 4:

TIME NEEDED: .... MINUTES

ACTIVITY: .... TO BE COMPLETED AT: ☐ HOME ☐ MEETING ☐ EVENT ☐ FIELD TRIP

PREP/SUPPLIES NEEDED: WHO'S RESPONSIBLE?

(1) .... ☐ LEADER ☐ GIRL/VOLUNTEER: ....

(2) .... ☐ LEADER ☐ GIRL/VOLUNTEER: ....

(3) .... ☐ LEADER ☐ GIRL/VOLUNTEER: ....

(4) .... ☐ LEADER ☐ GIRL/VOLUNTEER: ....

(5) .... ☐ LEADER ☐ GIRL/VOLUNTEER: ....

ACTIVITY STEPS/NOTES:

LEADERSHIP KEYS: ☐ DISCOVER ☐ CONNECT ☐ TAKE ACTION PROCESSES: ☐ GIRL-LED ☐ LEARNING BY DOING ☐ COOPERATIVE LEARNING

STEP 5:

TIME NEEDED: .... MINUTES

ACTIVITY: .... TO BE COMPLETED AT: ☐ HOME ☐ MEETING ☐ EVENT ☐ FIELD TRIP

PREP/SUPPLIES NEEDED: WHO'S RESPONSIBLE?

(1) .... ☐ LEADER ☐ GIRL/VOLUNTEER: ....

(2) .... ☐ LEADER ☐ GIRL/VOLUNTEER: ....

(3) .... ☐ LEADER ☐ GIRL/VOLUNTEER: ....

(4) .... ☐ LEADER ☐ GIRL/VOLUNTEER: ....

(5) .... ☐ LEADER ☐ GIRL/VOLUNTEER: ....

ACTIVITY STEPS/NOTES:

LEADERSHIP KEYS: ☐ DISCOVER ☐ CONNECT ☐ TAKE ACTION PROCESSES: ☐ GIRL-LED ☐ LEARNING BY DOING ☐ COOPERATIVE LEARNING

BADGE ACTIVITIES PLANNER

BADGE:

PURPOSE: ....

OF MEETINGS TO COMPLETE THIS BADGE: .... JOURNEY CONNECTION(S): .... ☐ STEP 1 ☐ STEP 2 ☐ STEP 3 ☐ STEP 4 ☐ STEP 5

LONG-TERM PLANNING:

FIELD TRIP/GUEST SPEAKER IDEAS:

STEP 1:

TIME NEEDED: .... MINUTES

ACTIVITY: .... TO BE COMPLETED AT: ☐ HOME ☐ MEETING ☐ EVENT ☐ FIELD TRIP

PREP/SUPPLIES NEEDED: WHO'S RESPONSIBLE?

(1) .... ☐ LEADER ☐ GIRL/VOLUNTEER: ....

(2) .... ☐ LEADER ☐ GIRL/VOLUNTEER: ....

(3) .... ☐ LEADER ☐ GIRL/VOLUNTEER: ....

(4) .... ☐ LEADER ☐ GIRL/VOLUNTEER: ....

(5) .... ☐ LEADER ☐ GIRL/VOLUNTEER: ....

ACTIVITY STEPS/NOTES:

LEADERSHIP KEYS: ☐ DISCOVER ☐ CONNECT ☐ TAKE ACTION PROCESSES: ☐ GIRL-LED ☐ LEARNING BY DOING ☐ COOPERATIVE LEARNING

STEP 2:

TIME NEEDED: .... MINUTES

ACTIVITY: .... TO BE COMPLETED AT: ☐ HOME ☐ MEETING ☐ EVENT ☐ FIELD TRIP

PREP/SUPPLIES NEEDED: WHO'S RESPONSIBLE?

(1) .... ☐ LEADER ☐ GIRL/VOLUNTEER: ....

(2) .... ☐ LEADER ☐ GIRL/VOLUNTEER: ....

(3) .... ☐ LEADER ☐ GIRL/VOLUNTEER: ....

(4) .... ☐ LEADER ☐ GIRL/VOLUNTEER: ....

(5) .... ☐ LEADER ☐ GIRL/VOLUNTEER: ....

ACTIVITY STEPS/NOTES:

LEADERSHIP KEYS: ☐ DISCOVER ☐ CONNECT ☐ TAKE ACTION PROCESSES: ☐ GIRL-LED ☐ LEARNING BY DOING ☐ COOPERATIVE LEARNING

STEP 3:

TIME NEEDED: .... MINUTES

ACTIVITY: .... TO BE COMPLETED AT: ☐ HOME ☐ MEETING ☐ EVENT ☐ FIELD TRIP

PREP/SUPPLIES NEEDED: WHO'S RESPONSIBLE?

(1) .... ☐ LEADER ☐ GIRL/VOLUNTEER: ....

(2) .... ☐ LEADER ☐ GIRL/VOLUNTEER: ....

(3) .... ☐ LEADER ☐ GIRL/VOLUNTEER: ....

(4) .... ☐ LEADER ☐ GIRL/VOLUNTEER: ....

(5) .... ☐ LEADER ☐ GIRL/VOLUNTEER: ....

ACTIVITY STEPS/NOTES:

LEADERSHIP KEYS: ☐ DISCOVER ☐ CONNECT ☐ TAKE ACTION PROCESSES: ☐ GIRL-LED ☐ LEARNING BY DOING ☐ COOPERATIVE LEARNING

STEP 4:

TIME NEEDED: .... MINUTES

ACTIVITY: .... TO BE COMPLETED AT: ☐ HOME ☐ MEETING ☐ EVENT ☐ FIELD TRIP

PREP/SUPPLIES NEEDED: WHO'S RESPONSIBLE?

(1) .... ☐ LEADER ☐ GIRL/VOLUNTEER: ....

(2) .... ☐ LEADER ☐ GIRL/VOLUNTEER: ....

(3) .... ☐ LEADER ☐ GIRL/VOLUNTEER: ....

(4) .... ☐ LEADER ☐ GIRL/VOLUNTEER: ....

(5) .... ☐ LEADER ☐ GIRL/VOLUNTEER: ....

ACTIVITY STEPS/NOTES:

LEADERSHIP KEYS: ☐ DISCOVER ☐ CONNECT ☐ TAKE ACTION PROCESSES: ☐ GIRL-LED ☐ LEARNING BY DOING ☐ COOPERATIVE LEARNING

STEP 5:

TIME NEEDED: .... MINUTES

ACTIVITY: .... TO BE COMPLETED AT: ☐ HOME ☐ MEETING ☐ EVENT ☐ FIELD TRIP

PREP/SUPPLIES NEEDED: WHO'S RESPONSIBLE?

(1) .... ☐ LEADER ☐ GIRL/VOLUNTEER: ....

(2) .... ☐ LEADER ☐ GIRL/VOLUNTEER: ....

(3) .... ☐ LEADER ☐ GIRL/VOLUNTEER: ....

(4) .... ☐ LEADER ☐ GIRL/VOLUNTEER: ....

(5) .... ☐ LEADER ☐ GIRL/VOLUNTEER: ....

ACTIVITY STEPS/NOTES:

LEADERSHIP KEYS: ☐ DISCOVER ☐ CONNECT ☐ TAKE ACTION PROCESSES: ☐ GIRL-LED ☐ LEARNING BY DOING ☐ COOPERATIVE LEARNING

TRACKER:

CUSTOMIZE THIS TRACKER TO MEET YOUR NEEDS! RECORD ATTENDANCE, DUES, BADGES, PRODUCT SALES, ETC.

TROOPS WITH 5-10 MEMBERS: LIST YOUR MEETINGS/DUES/PAPERWORK/BADGES/PRODUCTS IN THE FIRST COLUMN AND YOUR GIRL'S NAMES IN THE ANGLED COLUMN HEADERS.

TROOPS WITH 10+ MEMBERS: LIST YOUR GIRL'S NAMES IN THE FIRST COLUMN AND YOUR MEETINGS/DUES/PAPERWORK/BADGES/PRODUCTS IN THE ANGLED COLUMN HEADERS.

TRACKER:

CUSTOMIZE THIS TRACKER TO MEET YOUR NEEDS! RECORD ATTENDANCE, DUES, BADGES, PRODUCT SALES, ETC.

TROOPS WITH 5-10 MEMBERS: LIST YOUR MEETINGS/DUES/PAPERWORK/BADGES/PRODUCTS IN THE FIRST COLUMN AND YOUR GIRL'S NAMES IN THE ANGLED COLUMN HEADERS.

TROOPS WITH 10+ MEMBERS: LIST YOUR GIRL'S NAMES IN THE FIRST COLUMN AND YOUR MEETINGS/DUES/PAPERWORK/BADGES/PRODUCTS IN THE ANGLED COLUMN HEADERS.

TRACKER:

CUSTOMIZE THIS TRACKER TO MEET YOUR NEEDS! RECORD ATTENDANCE, DUES, BADGES, PRODUCT SALES, ETC.

TROOPS WITH 5-10 MEMBERS: LIST YOUR MEETINGS/DUES/PAPERWORK/BADGES/PRODUCTS IN THE FIRST COLUMN AND YOUR GIRL'S NAMES IN THE ANGLED COLUMN HEADERS.

TROOPS WITH 10+ MEMBERS: LIST YOUR GIRL'S NAMES IN THE FIRST COLUMN AND YOUR MEETINGS/DUES/PAPERWORK/BADGES/PRODUCTS IN THE ANGLED COLUMN HEADERS.

TRACKER:

CUSTOMIZE THIS TRACKER TO MEET YOUR NEEDS! RECORD ATTENDANCE, DUES, BADGES, PRODUCT SALES, ETC.

TROOPS WITH 5-10 MEMBERS: LIST YOUR MEETINGS/DUES/PAPERWORK/BADGES/PRODUCTS IN THE FIRST COLUMN AND YOUR GIRL'S NAMES IN THE ANGLED COLUMN HEADERS.

TROOPS WITH 10+ MEMBERS: LIST YOUR GIRL'S NAMES IN THE FIRST COLUMN AND YOUR MEETINGS/DUES/PAPERWORK/BADGES/PRODUCTS IN THE ANGLED COLUMN HEADERS.

TRACKER:

CUSTOMIZE THIS TRACKER TO MEET YOUR NEEDS! RECORD ATTENDANCE, DUES, BADGES, PRODUCT SALES, ETC.

TROOPS WITH 5-10 MEMBERS: LIST YOUR MEETINGS/DUES/PAPERWORK/BADGES/PRODUCTS IN THE FIRST COLUMN AND YOUR GIRL'S NAMES IN THE ANGLED COLUMN HEADERS.

TROOPS WITH 10+ MEMBERS: LIST YOUR GIRL'S NAMES IN THE FIRST COLUMN AND YOUR MEETINGS/DUES/PAPERWORK/BADGES/PRODUCTS IN THE ANGLED COLUMN HEADERS.

TRACKER:

CUSTOMIZE THIS TRACKER TO MEET YOUR NEEDS! RECORD ATTENDANCE, DUES, BADGES, PRODUCT SALES, ETC.

TROOPS WITH 5-10 MEMBERS: LIST YOUR MEETINGS/DUES/PAPERWORK/BADGES/PRODUCTS IN THE FIRST COLUMN AND YOUR GIRL'S NAMES IN THE ANGLED COLUMN HEADERS.

TROOPS WITH 10+ MEMBERS: LIST YOUR GIRL'S NAMES IN THE FIRST COLUMN AND YOUR MEETINGS/DUES/PAPERWORK/BADGES/PRODUCTS IN THE ANGLED COLUMN HEADERS.

TRACKER:

CUSTOMIZE THIS TRACKER TO MEET YOUR NEEDS! RECORD ATTENDANCE, DUES, BADGES, PRODUCT SALES, ETC.

TROOPS WITH 5-10 MEMBERS: LIST YOUR MEETINGS/DUES/PAPERWORK/BADGES/PRODUCTS IN THE FIRST COLUMN AND YOUR GIRL'S NAMES IN THE ANGLED COLUMN HEADERS.

TROOPS WITH 10+ MEMBERS: LIST YOUR GIRL'S NAMES IN THE FIRST COLUMN AND YOUR MEETINGS/DUES/PAPERWORK/BADGES/PRODUCTS IN THE ANGLED COLUMN HEADERS.

TRACKER:

CUSTOMIZE THIS TRACKER TO MEET YOUR NEEDS! RECORD ATTENDANCE, DUES, BADGES, PRODUCT SALES, ETC.

TROOPS WITH 5-10 MEMBERS: LIST YOUR MEETINGS/DUES/PAPERWORK/BADGES/PRODUCTS IN THE FIRST COLUMN AND YOUR GIRL'S NAMES IN THE ANGLED COLUMN HEADERS.

TROOPS WITH 10+ MEMBERS: LIST YOUR GIRL'S NAMES IN THE FIRST COLUMN AND YOUR MEETINGS/DUES/PAPERWORK/BADGES/PRODUCTS IN THE ANGLED COLUMN HEADERS.

TRACKER:

CUSTOMIZE THIS TRACKER TO MEET YOUR NEEDS! RECORD ATTENDANCE, DUES, BADGES, PRODUCT SALES, ETC.

TROOPS WITH 5-10 MEMBERS: LIST YOUR MEETINGS/DUES/PAPERWORK/BADGES/PRODUCTS IN THE FIRST COLUMN AND YOUR GIRL'S NAMES IN THE ANGLED COLUMN HEADERS.

TROOPS WITH 10+ MEMBERS: LIST YOUR GIRL'S NAMES IN THE FIRST COLUMN AND YOUR MEETINGS/DUES/PAPERWORK/BADGES/PRODUCTS IN THE ANGLED COLUMN HEADERS.

TRACKER:

CUSTOMIZE THIS TRACKER TO MEET YOUR NEEDS! RECORD ATTENDANCE, DUES, BADGES, PRODUCT SALES, ETC.

TROOPS WITH 5-10 MEMBERS: LIST YOUR MEETINGS/DUES/PAPERWORK/BADGES/PRODUCTS IN THE FIRST COLUMN AND YOUR GIRL'S NAMES IN THE ANGLED COLUMN HEADERS.

TROOPS WITH 10+ MEMBERS: LIST YOUR GIRL'S NAMES IN THE FIRST COLUMN AND YOUR MEETINGS/DUES/PAPERWORK/BADGES/PRODUCTS IN THE ANGLED COLUMN HEADERS.

TROOP DUES & BUDGET PLANNER

OF GIRLS:.......... # OF VOLUNTEERS:.......... # OF MEETINGS:.......... NOTES:

TROOP EXPENSES

TOTAL TROOP EXPENSES: $............................

PROGRAMS, EVENTS & FIELD TRIPS

(1)	$............ X .... = $............	(11)	$............ X .... = $............
(2)	$............ X .... = $............	(12)	$............ X .... = $............
(3)	$............ X .... = $............	(13)	$............ X .... = $............
(4)	$............ X .... = $............	(14)	$............ X .... = $............
(5)	$............ X .... = $............	(15)	$............ X .... = $............
(6)	$............ X .... = $............	(16)	$............ X .... = $............
(7)	$............ X .... = $............	(17)	$............ X .... = $............
(8)	$............ X .... = $............	(18)	$............ X .... = $............
(9)	$............ X .... = $............	(19)	$............ X .... = $............
(10)	$............ X .... = $............	(20)	$............ X .... = $............

TOTAL FOR PROGRAMS, EVENTS & FIELD TRIPS: $

UNIFORMS, BADGES & INSIGNIA

UNIFORMS	$............ X .... = $............	FUN PATCHES	$............ X .... = $............
GIRL SCOUTING GUIDES	$............ X .... = $............	OTHER:	$............ X .... = $............
JOURNEYS	$............ X .... = $............	OTHER:	$............ X .... = $............
BADGES	$............ X .... = $............	OTHER:	$............ X .... = $............

TOTAL FOR UNIFORMS, BADGES & INSIGNIA: $

SUPPLIES, SNACKS & OTHER EXPENSES

ANNUAL MEMBERSHIP FEES	$............ X .... = $............	COOKIE BOOTH SETUP	$............ X .... = $............
SERVICE UNIT DUES	$............ X .... = $............	CEREMONIES/CELEBRATIONS	$............ X .... = $............
ANNUAL FUND DONATIONS	$............ X .... = $............	CHARITABLE CONTRIBUTIONS	$............ X .... = $............
TROOP NECESSITIES	$............ X .... = $............	OTHER:	$............ X .... = $............
BADGE ACTIVITY SUPPLIES	$............ X .... = $............	OTHER:	$............ X .... = $............
SNACKS	$............ X .... = $............	OTHER:	$............ X .... = $............

TOTAL FOR SUPPLIES, SNACKS & OTHER EXPENSES: $

PARENT/GUARDIAN CONTRIBUTIONS

TOTAL PARENT/GUARDIAN CONTRIBUTIONS: $....................

PROGRAMS, EVENTS & FIELD TRIPS: $.................. FUN PATCHES: $.................. BADGE ACTIVITY SUPPLIES: $..................

UNIFORMS: $.................. ANNUAL MEMBERSHIP FEES: $.................. SNACKS: $..................

GIRL SCOUTING GUIDES: $.................. SERVICE UNIT DUES: $.................. COOKIE BOOTH SETUP: $..................

JOURNEYS: $.................. ANNUAL FUND DONATIONS: $.................. OTHER: ....

BADGES: $.................. TROOP NECESSITIES: $.................. OTHER: ....

TOTAL TROOP EXPENSES ($..............) MINUS TOTAL CONTRIBUTIONS FROM PARENTS/GUARDIANS ($..............) = REMAINING TROOP EXPENSES ($..............)

TROOP INCOME

TOTAL ESTIMATED TROOP INCOME: $....................

FALL PRODUCT SALES ☐ TROOP WILL PARTICIPATE ☐ TROOP WILL NOT PARTICIPATE

TROOP PROFIT PER SALE: .... # OF GIRLS PARTICIPATING: .... SALES REQUIRED TO COVER REMAINING TROOP EXPENSES: $........... ☐ ACHIEVABLE ☐ UNREALISTIC

TOTAL ESTIMATED FALL PRODUCT PROFIT: $.................. GROSS SALES OUR TROOP MUST MAKE TO ACHIEVE THIS ESTIMATED PROFIT: $..................

COOKIE SALES ☐ TROOP WILL PARTICIPATE ☐ TROOP WILL NOT PARTICIPATE

TROOP PROFIT PER BOX: $.......... # OF GIRLS PARTICIPATING: .... SALES REQUIRED TO COVER REMAINING TROOP EXPENSES: .... ☐ ACHIEVEABLE ☐ UNREALISTIC

TOTAL ESTIMATED COOKIE PROFIT: $.................. # OF BOXES OUR TROOP MUST SELL TO ACHIEVE THIS ESTIMATED PROFIT: ....

OTHER COUNCIL-APPROVED MONEY-EARNING ACTIVITIES ☐ TROOP WILL PARTICIPATE ☐ TROOP WILL NOT PARTICIPATE

(1) : $.................. (2) : $.................. (3) : $..................

TOTAL ESTIMATED PROFIT FROM OTHER COUNCIL-APPROVED MONEY-EARNING ACTIVITIES: $..................

TROOP DUES

STARTING ACCOUNT BALANCE: $.............. ☐ 100% IS RESERVED FOR A TRIP, ETC. ☐ 100% CAN BE USED TO COVER EXPENSES ☐ $.......... CAN BE USED TO COVER EXPENSES

TROOP DUES CALCULATOR:

$...................... + $...................... + $...................... = $...................... - $...................... = $......................

AVAILABLE FUNDS FROM ACCOUNT BALANCE	PARENT/GUARDIAN CONTRIBUTIONS	TOTAL ESTIMATED TROOP INCOME		TOTAL TROOP EXPENSES	TOTAL TROOP DUES

TOTAL TROOP DUES ($..............) DIVIDED BY THE NUMBER OF GIRLS (.........) = TROOP DUES PER GIRL ($..............)

TROOP DUES WILL BE COLLECTED ☐ UPFRONT ☐ AT EACH MEETING (TROOP DUES PER GIRL DIVIDED BY # OF MEETINGS = $.............)

NOTES:

TROOP FINANCES

CHECKING ACCOUNT DETAILS

STARTING BALANCE AS OF ..../......./....... : $......................

BANK: .... LOCATION: .... HOURS: ....

ACCOUNT NUMBER: .... ROUTING NUMBER: .... DEBIT CARD NUMBER: .... CVV: ....

NOTES:

DATE	CHECK/DEBIT	DESCRIPTION	WITHDRAWAL	DEPOSIT	BALANCE
	☐ CHECK # ☐ DEBIT CARD				
	☐ CHECK # ☐ DEBIT CARD				
	☐ CHECK # ☐ DEBIT CARD				
	☐ CHECK # ☐ DEBIT CARD				
	☐ CHECK # ☐ DEBIT CARD				
	☐ CHECK # ☐ DEBIT CARD				
	☐ CHECK # ☐ DEBIT CARD				
	☐ CHECK # ☐ DEBIT CARD				
	☐ CHECK # ☐ DEBIT CARD				
	☐ CHECK # ☐ DEBIT CARD				
	☐ CHECK # ☐ DEBIT CARD				
	☐ CHECK # ☐ DEBIT CARD				
	☐ CHECK # ☐ DEBIT CARD				
	☐ CHECK # ☐ DEBIT CARD				
	☐ CHECK # ☐ DEBIT CARD				
	☐ CHECK # ☐ DEBIT CARD				
	☐ CHECK # ☐ DEBIT CARD				
	☐ CHECK # ☐ DEBIT CARD				
	☐ CHECK # ☐ DEBIT CARD				
	☐ CHECK # ☐ DEBIT CARD				

"When I dare to be powerful... then it becomes less and less important whether I am afraid."

AUTHOR & ACTIVIST AUDRE LORDE

DATE	CHECK/DEBIT	DESCRIPTION	WITHDRAWAL	DEPOSIT	BALANCE
	☐ CHECK # ☐ DEBIT CARD				
	☐ CHECK # ☐ DEBIT CARD				
	☐ CHECK # ☐ DEBIT CARD				
	☐ CHECK # ☐ DEBIT CARD				
	☐ CHECK # ☐ DEBIT CARD				
	☐ CHECK # ☐ DEBIT CARD				
	☐ CHECK # ☐ DEBIT CARD				
	☐ CHECK # ☐ DEBIT CARD				
	☐ CHECK # ☐ DEBIT CARD				
	☐ CHECK # ☐ DEBIT CARD				
	☐ CHECK # ☐ DEBIT CARD				
	☐ CHECK # ☐ DEBIT CARD				
	☐ CHECK # ☐ DEBIT CARD				
	☐ CHECK # ☐ DEBIT CARD				
	☐ CHECK # ☐ DEBIT CARD				
	☐ CHECK # ☐ DEBIT CARD				
	☐ CHECK # ☐ DEBIT CARD				
	☐ CHECK # ☐ DEBIT CARD				
	☐ CHECK # ☐ DEBIT CARD				
	☐ CHECK # ☐ DEBIT CARD				
	☐ CHECK # ☐ DEBIT CARD				
	☐ CHECK # ☐ DEBIT CARD				
	☐ CHECK # ☐ DEBIT CARD				
	☐ CHECK # ☐ DEBIT CARD				

TROOP LEADER TAX-DEDUCTIBLE EXPENSES

DATE	EXPENSE	COST	DATE	EXPENSE	COST

TROOP LEADER TAX-DEDUCTIBLE MILEAGE

DATE	PURPOSE	MILES	DATE	PURPOSE	MILES

COOKIE BOOTH PLANNER

TROOP COOKIE MANAGER(S): ....

COOKIE BOOTH NOTES:

DATE & TIME	COOKIE BOOTH LOCATION	VOLUNTEERS	GIRLS	
		(1)	(1)	(3)
M T W TH F SAT SUN		(2)	(2)	(4)
		(1)	(1)	(3)
M T W TH F SAT SUN		(2)	(2)	(4)
		(1)	(1)	(3)
M T W TH F SAT SUN		(2)	(2)	(4)
		(1)	(1)	(3)
M T W TH F SAT SUN		(2)	(2)	(4)
		(1)	(1)	(3)
M T W TH F SAT SUN		(2)	(2)	(4)
		(1)	(1)	(3)
M T W TH F SAT SUN		(2)	(2)	(4)
		(1)	(1)	(3)
M T W TH F SAT SUN		(2)	(2)	(4)
		(1)	(1)	(3)
M T W TH F SAT SUN		(2)	(2)	(4)

"Growth is not merely a harmonious increase in size but a transformation."

EDUCATION PIONEER MARIA MONTESSORI

COOKIE BOOTH NOTES:

DATE & TIME	COOKIE BOOTH LOCATION	VOLUNTEERS	GIRLS	
M T W TH F SAT SUN		(1) (2)	(1) (2)	(3) (4)
M T W TH F SAT SUN		(1) (2)	(1) (2)	(3) (4)
M T W TH F SAT SUN		(1) (2)	(1) (2)	(3) (4)
M T W TH F SAT SUN		(1) (2)	(1) (2)	(3) (4)
M T W TH F SAT SUN		(1) (2)	(1) (2)	(3) (4)
M T W TH F SAT SUN		(1) (2)	(1) (2)	(3) (4)
M T W TH F SAT SUN		(1) (2)	(1) (2)	(3) (4)
M T W TH F SAT SUN		(1) (2)	(1) (2)	(3) (4)

COOKIE BOOTH SALES TRACKER

COOKIE BOOTH LOCATION:

TOTAL CASH & CREDIT CARD SALES: $........................

DATE: ...../......./...... STARTING TIME:.............. ENDING TIME:.............. VOLUNTEERS:...

	PRICE PER BOX	STARTING # OF BOXES	ENDING # OF BOXES	BOXES SOLD	CASH SALES	CREDIT CARD SALES
THIN MINTS	$				$	$
SAMOAS / CARAMEL DELITES	$				$	$
TAGALONGS / PEANUT BUTTER PATTIES	$				$	$
TREFOILS / SHORTBREAD	$				$	$
DO-SI-DOS / PEANUT BUTTER SANDWICH	$				$	$
SAVANNAH SMILES	$				$	$
TOFFEE-TASTIC	$				$	$
THANKS-A-LOT	$				$	$
S'MORES	$				$	$
LEMONADES	$				$	$
CARAMEL CHOCOLATE CHIP	$				$	$

TOTALS: .... STARTING # OF BOXES .... ENDING # OF BOXES .... BOXES SOLD $........................ CASH SALES $........................ CREDIT CARD SALES

STARTING # OF BOXES (..........) MINUS ENDING # OF BOXES (..........) = TOTAL BOXES SOLD (..........) ☐ SAME AS ABOVE (YAY!) ☐ DIFFERENT FROM ABOVE (UH-OH)

ENDING CASH ($.............) MINUS STARTING CASH ($.............) = TOTAL CASH SALES ($.............) ☐ SAME AS ABOVE (YAY!) ☐ DIFFERENT FROM ABOVE (UH-OH)

COOKIE BOOTH HOURS

GIRL	START TIME	END TIME	TOTAL HOURS	BOXES SOLD	GIRL	START TIME	END TIME	TOTAL HOURS	BOXES SOLD

NOTES:

TOTAL ESTIMATED TROOP PROFIT FROM THIS COOKIE BOOTH: $....................

"This is what my soul is telling me: Be peaceful and love everyone."
NOBEL PRIZE LAUREATE MALALA YOUSAFZI

COOKIE BOOTH LOCATION:

TOTAL CASH & CREDIT CARD SALES: $.......................

DATE: ...../......./....... STARTING TIME:.............. ENDING TIME:.............. VOLUNTEERS:..

	PRICE PER BOX	STARTING # OF BOXES	ENDING # OF BOXES	BOXES SOLD	CASH SALES	CREDIT CARD SALES
THIN MINTS	$				$	$
SAMOAS / CARAMEL DELITES	$				$	$
TAGALONGS / PEANUT BUTTER PATTIES	$				$	$
TREFOILS / SHORTBREAD	$				$	$
DO-SI-DOS / PEANUT BUTTER SANDWICH	$				$	$
SAVANNAH SMILES	$				$	$
TOFFEE-TASTIC	$				$	$
THANKS-A-LOT	$				$	$
S'MORES	$				$	$
LEMONADES	$				$	$
CARAMEL CHOCOLATE CHIP	$				$	$

TOTALS:	....	....	....	$........................	$........................
	STARTING # OF BOXES	ENDING # OF BOXES	BOXES SOLD	CASH SALES	CREDIT CARD SALES

STARTING # OF BOXES (..........) MINUS ENDING # OF BOXES (..........) = TOTAL BOXES SOLD (..........) ☐ SAME AS ABOVE (YAY!) ☐ DIFFERENT FROM ABOVE (UH-OH)

ENDING CASH ($.............) MINUS STARTING CASH ($.............) = TOTAL CASH SALES ($.............) ☐ SAME AS ABOVE (YAY!) ☐ DIFFERENT FROM ABOVE (UH-OH)

COOKIE BOOTH HOURS

GIRL	START TIME	END TIME	TOTAL HOURS	BOXES SOLD	GIRL	START TIME	END TIME	TOTAL HOURS	BOXES SOLD

OTES:

TOTAL ESTIMATED TROOP PROFIT FROM THIS COOKIE BOOTH: $.....................

COOKIE BOOTH SALES TRACKER

COOKIE BOOTH LOCATION:

TOTAL CASH & CREDIT CARD SALES: $......................

DATE: ...../......./...... STARTING TIME:............. ENDING TIME:............. VOLUNTEERS:..

	PRICE PER BOX	STARTING # OF BOXES	ENDING # OF BOXES	BOXES SOLD	CASH SALES	CREDIT CARD SALES
THIN MINTS	$				$	$
SAMOAS / CARAMEL DELITES	$				$	$
TAGALONGS / PEANUT BUTTER PATTIES	$				$	$
TREFOILS / SHORTBREAD	$				$	$
DO-SI-DOS / PEANUT BUTTER SANDWICH	$				$	$
SAVANNAH SMILES	$				$	$
TOFFEE-TASTIC	$				$	$
THANKS-A-LOT	$				$	$
S'MORES	$				$	$
LEMONADES	$				$	$
CARAMEL CHOCOLATE CHIP	$				$	$

TOTALS:	....	....	....	$........................	$........................
	STARTING # OF BOXES	ENDING # OF BOXES	BOXES SOLD	CASH SALES	CREDIT CARD SALES

STARTING # OF BOXES (..........) MINUS ENDING # OF BOXES (..........) = TOTAL BOXES SOLD (..........) ☐ SAME AS ABOVE (YAY!) ☐ DIFFERENT FROM ABOVE (UH-OH)

ENDING CASH ($............) MINUS STARTING CASH ($............) = TOTAL CASH SALES ($............) ☐ SAME AS ABOVE (YAY!) ☐ DIFFERENT FROM ABOVE (UH-OH)

COOKIE BOOTH HOURS

GIRL	START TIME	END TIME	TOTAL HOURS	BOXES SOLD	GIRL	START TIME	END TIME	TOTAL HOURS	BOXES SOLD

NOTES:

TOTAL ESTIMATED TROOP PROFIT FROM THIS COOKIE BOOTH: $....................

"There's a big wonderful world out there for you. ... Don't cheat yourself out of this promise."
FORMER FIRST LADY NANCY REAGAN

COOKIE BOOTH LOCATION:

TOTAL CASH & CREDIT CARD SALES: $..................

DATE: ..../...../..... STARTING TIME:............ ENDING TIME:............ VOLUNTEERS:..................

	PRICE PER BOX	STARTING # OF BOXES	ENDING # OF BOXES	BOXES SOLD	CASH SALES	CREDIT CARD SALES
THIN MINTS	$				$	$
SAMOAS / CARAMEL DELITES	$				$	$
TAGALONGS / PEANUT BUTTER PATTIES	$				$	$
TREFOILS / SHORTBREAD	$				$	$
DO-SI-DOS / PEANUT BUTTER SANDWICH	$				$	$
SAVANNAH SMILES	$				$	$
TOFFEE-TASTIC	$				$	$
THANKS-A-LOT	$				$	$
S'MORES	$				$	$
LEMONADES	$				$	$
CARAMEL CHOCOLATE CHIP	$				$	$

TOTALS: .... STARTING # OF BOXES .... ENDING # OF BOXES .... BOXES SOLD $.............. CASH SALES $.............. CREDIT CARD SALES

STARTING # OF BOXES (..........) MINUS ENDING # OF BOXES (..........) = TOTAL BOXES SOLD (..........) ☐ SAME AS ABOVE (YAY!) ☐ DIFFERENT FROM ABOVE (UH-OH)

ENDING CASH ($............) MINUS STARTING CASH ($............) = TOTAL CASH SALES ($............) ☐ SAME AS ABOVE (YAY!) ☐ DIFFERENT FROM ABOVE (UH-OH)

COOKIE BOOTH HOURS

GIRL	START TIME	END TIME	TOTAL HOURS	BOXES SOLD	GIRL	START TIME	END TIME	TOTAL HOURS	BOXES SOLD

NOTES:

TOTAL ESTIMATED TROOP PROFIT FROM THIS COOKIE BOOTH: $..................

COOKIE BOOTH SALES TRACKER

COOKIE BOOTH LOCATION:

TOTAL CASH & CREDIT CARD SALES: $ ....

DATE: ...../......./....... STARTING TIME:.............. ENDING TIME:.............. VOLUNTEERS:..

	PRICE PER BOX	STARTING # OF BOXES	ENDING # OF BOXES	BOXES SOLD	CASH SALES	CREDIT CARD SALES
THIN MINTS	$				$	$
SAMOAS / CARAMEL DELITES	$				$	$
TAGALONGS / PEANUT BUTTER PATTIES	$				$	$
TREFOILS / SHORTBREAD	$				$	$
DO-SI-DOS / PEANUT BUTTER SANDWICH	$				$	$
SAVANNAH SMILES	$				$	$
TOFFEE-TASTIC	$				$	$
THANKS-A-LOT	$				$	$
S'MORES	$				$	$
LEMONADES	$				$	$
CARAMEL CHOCOLATE CHIP	$				$	$

TOTALS: .... STARTING # OF BOXES .... ENDING # OF BOXES .... BOXES SOLD $.......................... CASH SALES $.......................... CREDIT CARD SALES

STARTING # OF BOXES (..........) MINUS ENDING # OF BOXES (..........) = TOTAL BOXES SOLD (..........) ☐ SAME AS ABOVE (YAY!) ☐ DIFFERENT FROM ABOVE (UH-OH)

ENDING CASH ($.............) MINUS STARTING CASH ($.............) = TOTAL CASH SALES ($.............) ☐ SAME AS ABOVE (YAY!) ☐ DIFFERENT FROM ABOVE (UH-OH)

COOKIE BOOTH HOURS

GIRL	START TIME	END TIME	TOTAL HOURS	BOXES SOLD	GIRL	START TIME	END TIME	TOTAL HOURS	BOXES SOLD

NOTES:

TOTAL ESTIMATED TROOP PROFIT FROM THIS COOKIE BOOTH: $.....................

"Nothing happens in the 'real' world unless it first happens in the images in our heads."

AMERICAN SCHOLAR GLORIA ANZALDUA

COOKIE BOOTH LOCATION:

TOTAL CASH & CREDIT CARD SALES: $..................

DATE: ...../....../...... STARTING TIME:.............. ENDING TIME:.............. VOLUNTEERS:..

	PRICE PER BOX	STARTING # OF BOXES	ENDING # OF BOXES	BOXES SOLD	CASH SALES	CREDIT CARD SALES
THIN MINTS	$				$	$
SAMOAS / CARAMEL DELITES	$				$	$
TAGALONGS / PEANUT BUTTER PATTIES	$				$	$
TREFOILS / SHORTBREAD	$				$	$
DO-SI-DOS / PEANUT BUTTER SANDWICH	$				$	$
SAVANNAH SMILES	$				$	$
TOFFEE-TASTIC	$				$	$
THANKS-A-LOT	$				$	$
S'MORES	$				$	$
LEMONADES	$				$	$
CARAMEL CHOCOLATE CHIP	$				$	$

TOTALS: .... STARTING # OF BOXES .... ENDING # OF BOXES .... BOXES SOLD $.................. CASH SALES $.................. CREDIT CARD SALES

STARTING # OF BOXES (..........) MINUS ENDING # OF BOXES (..........) = TOTAL BOXES SOLD (..........) ☐ SAME AS ABOVE (YAY!) ☐ DIFFERENT FROM ABOVE (UH-OH)

ENDING CASH ($............) MINUS STARTING CASH ($............) = TOTAL CASH SALES ($............) ☐ SAME AS ABOVE (YAY!) ☐ DIFFERENT FROM ABOVE (UH-OH)

COOKIE BOOTH HOURS

GIRL	START TIME	END TIME	TOTAL HOURS	BOXES SOLD	GIRL	START TIME	END TIME	TOTAL HOURS	BOXES SOLD

NOTES:

TOTAL ESTIMATED TROOP PROFIT FROM THIS COOKIE BOOTH: $..................

COOKIE BOOTH SALES TRACKER

COOKIE BOOTH LOCATION:

TOTAL CASH & CREDIT CARD SALES: $..................

DATE: ..../....../...... STARTING TIME:............ ENDING TIME:............ VOLUNTEERS:..

	PRICE PER BOX	STARTING # OF BOXES	ENDING # OF BOXES	BOXES SOLD	CASH SALES	CREDIT CARD SALES
THIN MINTS	$				$	$
SAMOAS / CARAMEL DELITES	$				$	$
TAGALONGS / PEANUT BUTTER PATTIES	$				$	$
TREFOILS / SHORTBREAD	$				$	$
DO-SI-DOS / PEANUT BUTTER SANDWICH	$				$	$
SAVANNAH SMILES	$				$	$
TOFFEE-TASTIC	$				$	$
THANKS-A-LOT	$				$	$
S'MORES	$				$	$
LEMONADES	$				$	$
CARAMEL CHOCOLATE CHIP	$				$	$

TOTALS: .... STARTING # OF BOXES .... ENDING # OF BOXES .... BOXES SOLD $.................. CASH SALES $.................. CREDIT CARD SALES

STARTING # OF BOXES (.........) MINUS ENDING # OF BOXES (.........) = TOTAL BOXES SOLD (.........) ☐ SAME AS ABOVE (YAY!) ☐ DIFFERENT FROM ABOVE (UH-OH)

ENDING CASH ($............) MINUS STARTING CASH ($............) = TOTAL CASH SALES ($............) ☐ SAME AS ABOVE (YAY!) ☐ DIFFERENT FROM ABOVE (UH-OH)

COOKIE BOOTH HOURS

GIRL	START TIME	END TIME	TOTAL HOURS	BOXES SOLD	GIRL	START TIME	END TIME	TOTAL HOURS	BOXES SOLD

NOTES:

TOTAL ESTIMATED TROOP PROFIT FROM THIS COOKIE BOOTH: $..................

"I did what my conscience told me to do, and you can't fail if you do that."
ATTORNEY & ACADEMIC ANITA HILL

COOKIE BOOTH LOCATION:

TOTAL CASH & CREDIT CARD SALES: $.....................

DATE: ..../....../...... STARTING TIME:............ ENDING TIME:............ VOLUNTEERS:..

	PRICE PER BOX	STARTING # OF BOXES	ENDING # OF BOXES	BOXES SOLD	CASH SALES	CREDIT CARD SALES
THIN MINTS	$				$	$
SAMOAS / CARAMEL DELITES	$				$	$
TAGALONGS / PEANUT BUTTER PATTIES	$				$	$
TREFOILS / SHORTBREAD	$				$	$
DO-SI-DOS / PEANUT BUTTER SANDWICH	$				$	$
SAVANNAH SMILES	$				$	$
TOFFEE-TASTIC	$				$	$
THANKS-A-LOT	$				$	$
S'MORES	$				$	$
LEMONADES	$				$	$
CARAMEL CHOCOLATE CHIP	$				$	$

TOTALS: .... STARTING # OF BOXES .... ENDING # OF BOXES .... BOXES SOLD $.................... CASH SALES $.................... CREDIT CARD SALES

STARTING # OF BOXES (..........) MINUS ENDING # OF BOXES (..........) = TOTAL BOXES SOLD (..........) ☐ SAME AS ABOVE (YAY!) ☐ DIFFERENT FROM ABOVE (UH-OH)

ENDING CASH ($............) MINUS STARTING CASH ($............) = TOTAL CASH SALES ($............) ☐ SAME AS ABOVE (YAY!) ☐ DIFFERENT FROM ABOVE (UH-OH)

COOKIE BOOTH HOURS

GIRL	START TIME	END TIME	TOTAL HOURS	BOXES SOLD	GIRL	START TIME	END TIME	TOTAL HOURS	BOXES SOLD

NOTES:

TOTAL ESTIMATED TROOP PROFIT FROM THIS COOKIE BOOTH: $....................

COOKIE BOOTH SALES TRACKER

COOKIE BOOTH LOCATION:

TOTAL CASH & CREDIT CARD SALES: $ ....

DATE: ...../...../..... STARTING TIME:............. ENDING TIME:............. VOLUNTEERS:..

	PRICE PER BOX	STARTING # OF BOXES	ENDING # OF BOXES	BOXES SOLD	CASH SALES	CREDIT CARD SALES
THIN MINTS	$				$	$
SAMOAS / CARAMEL DELITES	$				$	$
TAGALONGS / PEANUT BUTTER PATTIES	$				$	$
TREFOILS / SHORTBREAD	$				$	$
DO-SI-DOS / PEANUT BUTTER SANDWICH	$				$	$
SAVANNAH SMILES	$				$	$
TOFFEE-TASTIC	$				$	$
THANKS-A-LOT	$				$	$
S'MORES	$				$	$
LEMONADES	$				$	$
CARAMEL CHOCOLATE CHIP	$				$	$

TOTALS: .... STARTING # OF BOXES .... ENDING # OF BOXES .... BOXES SOLD $.................... CASH SALES $.................... CREDIT CARD SALES

STARTING # OF BOXES (..........) MINUS ENDING # OF BOXES (..........) = TOTAL BOXES SOLD (..........) ☐ SAME AS ABOVE (YAY!) ☐ DIFFERENT FROM ABOVE (UH-OH)

ENDING CASH ($............) MINUS STARTING CASH ($............) = TOTAL CASH SALES ($............) ☐ SAME AS ABOVE (YAY!) ☐ DIFFERENT FROM ABOVE (UH-OH)

COOKIE BOOTH HOURS

GIRL	START TIME	END TIME	TOTAL HOURS	BOXES SOLD	GIRL	START TIME	END TIME	TOTAL HOURS	BOXES SOLD

NOTES:

TOTAL ESTIMATED TROOP PROFIT FROM THIS COOKIE BOOTH: $....................

"There are still many causes worth sacrificing for, so much history still yet to be made."

FORMER FIRST LADY MICHELLE OBAMA

COOKIE BOOTH LOCATION:

TOTAL CASH & CREDIT CARD SALES: $ ....

DATE: ...../....../...... STARTING TIME:............. ENDING TIME:............. VOLUNTEERS:..

	PRICE PER BOX	STARTING # OF BOXES	ENDING # OF BOXES	BOXES SOLD	CASH SALES	CREDIT CARD SALES
THIN MINTS	$				$	$
SAMOAS / CARAMEL DELITES	$				$	$
TAGALONGS / PEANUT BUTTER PATTIES	$				$	$
TREFOILS / SHORTBREAD	$				$	$
DO-SI-DOS / PEANUT BUTTER SANDWICH	$				$	$
SAVANNAH SMILES	$				$	$
TOFFEE-TASTIC	$				$	$
THANKS-A-LOT	$				$	$
S'MORES	$				$	$
LEMONADES	$				$	$
CARAMEL CHOCOLATE CHIP	$				$	$

TOTALS:	....	....	....	$....................	$....................
	STARTING # OF BOXES	ENDING # OF BOXES	BOXES SOLD	CASH SALES	CREDIT CARD SALES

STARTING # OF BOXES (..........) MINUS ENDING # OF BOXES (..........) = TOTAL BOXES SOLD (..........) ☐ SAME AS ABOVE (YAY!) ☐ DIFFERENT FROM ABOVE (UH-OH)

ENDING CASH ($............) MINUS STARTING CASH ($............) = TOTAL CASH SALES ($............) ☐ SAME AS ABOVE (YAY!) ☐ DIFFERENT FROM ABOVE (UH-OH)

COOKIE BOOTH HOURS

GIRL	START TIME	END TIME	TOTAL HOURS	BOXES SOLD	GIRL	START TIME	END TIME	TOTAL HOURS	BOXES SOLD

NOTES:

TOTAL ESTIMATED TROOP PROFIT FROM THIS COOKIE BOOTH: $....................

VOLUNTEER SIGN-UP

THANK YOU!

NOTES FOR VOLUNTEERS:

DATE & TIME	MEETING / EVENT	# OF VOLUNTEERS NEEDED	VOLUNTEER NAMES & PHONE NUMBERS
M T W TH F SAT SUN	☐ MEETING ☐ COOKIE BOOTH ☐ EVENT:		
M T W TH F SAT SUN	☐ MEETING ☐ COOKIE BOOTH ☐ EVENT:		
M T W TH F SAT SUN	☐ MEETING ☐ COOKIE BOOTH ☐ EVENT:		
M T W TH F SAT SUN	☐ MEETING ☐ COOKIE BOOTH ☐ EVENT:		
M T W TH F SAT SUN	☐ MEETING ☐ COOKIE BOOTH ☐ EVENT:		
M T W TH F SAT SUN	☐ MEETING ☐ COOKIE BOOTH ☐ EVENT:		
M T W TH F SAT SUN	☐ MEETING ☐ COOKIE BOOTH ☐ EVENT:		
M T W TH F SAT SUN	☐ MEETING ☐ COOKIE BOOTH ☐ EVENT:		

"Knowing what needs to be done does away with fear."
CIVIL RIGHTS ACTIVIST ROSA PARKS

NOTES FOR VOLUNTEERS:

DATE & TIME	MEETING / EVENT	# OF VOLUNTEERS NEEDED	VOLUNTEER NAMES & PHONE NUMBERS
M T W TH F SAT SUN	☐ MEETING ☐ COOKIE BOOTH ☐ EVENT:		
M T W TH F SAT SUN	☐ MEETING ☐ COOKIE BOOTH ☐ EVENT:		
M T W TH F SAT SUN	☐ MEETING ☐ COOKIE BOOTH ☐ EVENT:		
M T W TH F SAT SUN	☐ MEETING ☐ COOKIE BOOTH ☐ EVENT:		
M T W TH F SAT SUN	☐ MEETING ☐ COOKIE BOOTH ☐ EVENT:		
M T W TH F SAT SUN	☐ MEETING ☐ COOKIE BOOTH ☐ EVENT:		
M T W TH F SAT SUN	☐ MEETING ☐ COOKIE BOOTH ☐ EVENT:		
M T W TH F SAT SUN	☐ MEETING ☐ COOKIE BOOTH ☐ EVENT:		

VOLUNTEER SIGN-UP

THANK YOU!

NOTES FOR VOLUNTEERS:

DATE & TIME	MEETING / EVENT	# OF VOLUNTEERS NEEDED	VOLUNTEER NAMES & PHONE NUMBERS
M T W TH F SAT SUN	☐ MEETING ☐ COOKIE BOOTH ☐ EVENT:		
M T W TH F SAT SUN	☐ MEETING ☐ COOKIE BOOTH ☐ EVENT:		
M T W TH F SAT SUN	☐ MEETING ☐ COOKIE BOOTH ☐ EVENT:		
M T W TH F SAT SUN	☐ MEETING ☐ COOKIE BOOTH ☐ EVENT:		
M T W TH F SAT SUN	☐ MEETING ☐ COOKIE BOOTH ☐ EVENT:		
M T W TH F SAT SUN	☐ MEETING ☐ COOKIE BOOTH ☐ EVENT:		
M T W TH F SAT SUN	☐ MEETING ☐ COOKIE BOOTH ☐ EVENT:		
M T W TH F SAT SUN	☐ MEETING ☐ COOKIE BOOTH ☐ EVENT:		

"Learn from the mistakes of others. You can't live long enough to make them all yourself."
FORMER FIRST LADY ELEANOR ROOSEVELT

NOTES FOR VOLUNTEERS:

DATE & TIME	MEETING / EVENT	# OF VOLUNTEERS NEEDED	VOLUNTEER NAMES & PHONE NUMBERS
M T W TH F SAT SUN	☐ MEETING ☐ COOKIE BOOTH ☐ EVENT:		
M T W TH F SAT SUN	☐ MEETING ☐ COOKIE BOOTH ☐ EVENT:		
M T W TH F SAT SUN	☐ MEETING ☐ COOKIE BOOTH ☐ EVENT:		
M T W TH F SAT SUN	☐ MEETING ☐ COOKIE BOOTH ☐ EVENT:		
M T W TH F SAT SUN	☐ MEETING ☐ COOKIE BOOTH ☐ EVENT:		
M T W TH F SAT SUN	☐ MEETING ☐ COOKIE BOOTH ☐ EVENT:		
M T W TH F SAT SUN	☐ MEETING ☐ COOKIE BOOTH ☐ EVENT:		
M T W TH F SAT SUN	☐ MEETING ☐ COOKIE BOOTH ☐ EVENT:		

VOLUNTEER SIGN-UP

THANK YOU!

NOTES FOR VOLUNTEERS:

DATE & TIME	MEETING / EVENT	# OF VOLUNTEERS NEEDED	VOLUNTEER NAMES & PHONE NUMBERS
M T W TH F SAT SUN	☐ MEETING ☐ COOKIE BOOTH ☐ EVENT:		
M T W TH F SAT SUN	☐ MEETING ☐ COOKIE BOOTH ☐ EVENT:		
M T W TH F SAT SUN	☐ MEETING ☐ COOKIE BOOTH ☐ EVENT:		
M T W TH F SAT SUN	☐ MEETING ☐ COOKIE BOOTH ☐ EVENT:		
M T W TH F SAT SUN	☐ MEETING ☐ COOKIE BOOTH ☐ EVENT:		
M T W TH F SAT SUN	☐ MEETING ☐ COOKIE BOOTH ☐ EVENT:		
M T W TH F SAT SUN	☐ MEETING ☐ COOKIE BOOTH ☐ EVENT:		
M T W TH F SAT SUN	☐ MEETING ☐ COOKIE BOOTH ☐ EVENT:		

"A good compromise is one where everybody makes a contribution."

CHANCELLOR OF GERMANY ANGELA MERKEL

NOTES FOR VOLUNTEERS:

DATE & TIME	MEETING / EVENT	# OF VOLUNTEERS NEEDED	VOLUNTEER NAMES & PHONE NUMBERS
M T W TH F SAT SUN	☐ MEETING ☐ COOKIE BOOTH ☐ EVENT:		
M T W TH F SAT SUN	☐ MEETING ☐ COOKIE BOOTH ☐ EVENT:		
M T W TH F SAT SUN	☐ MEETING ☐ COOKIE BOOTH ☐ EVENT:		
M T W TH F SAT SUN	☐ MEETING ☐ COOKIE BOOTH ☐ EVENT:		
M T W TH F SAT SUN	☐ MEETING ☐ COOKIE BOOTH ☐ EVENT:		
M T W TH F SAT SUN	☐ MEETING ☐ COOKIE BOOTH ☐ EVENT:		
M T W TH F SAT SUN	☐ MEETING ☐ COOKIE BOOTH ☐ EVENT:		
M T W TH F SAT SUN	☐ MEETING ☐ COOKIE BOOTH ☐ EVENT:		

SNACK SIGN-UP

THANK YOU!

SNACK SUGGESTIONS:

INGREDIENTS TO AVOID:

PLEASE BRING SNACKS FOR .... PEOPLE.

DATE	MEETING / EVENT	VOLUNTEER NAME & PHONE NUMBER
	☐ MEETING ☐ EVENT:	
	☐ MEETING ☐ EVENT:	
	☐ MEETING ☐ EVENT:	
	☐ MEETING ☐ EVENT:	
	☐ MEETING ☐ EVENT:	
	☐ MEETING ☐ EVENT:	
	☐ MEETING ☐ EVENT:	
	☐ MEETING ☐ EVENT:	
	☐ MEETING ☐ EVENT:	
	☐ MEETING ☐ EVENT:	
	☐ MEETING ☐ EVENT:	
	☐ MEETING ☐ EVENT:	
	☐ MEETING ☐ EVENT:	

SNACK SIGN-UP

THANK YOU!

SNACK SUGGESTIONS:

INGREDIENTS TO AVOID:

PLEASE BRING SNACKS FOR .... PEOPLE.

DATE	MEETING / EVENT	VOLUNTEER NAME & PHONE NUMBER
	☐ MEETING ☐ EVENT:	
	☐ MEETING ☐ EVENT:	
	☐ MEETING ☐ EVENT:	
	☐ MEETING ☐ EVENT:	
	☐ MEETING ☐ EVENT:	
	☐ MEETING ☐ EVENT:	
	☐ MEETING ☐ EVENT:	
	☐ MEETING ☐ EVENT:	
	☐ MEETING ☐ EVENT:	
	☐ MEETING ☐ EVENT:	
	☐ MEETING ☐ EVENT:	
	☐ MEETING ☐ EVENT:	
	☐ MEETING ☐ EVENT:	

VOLUNTEER DRIVER LOG

NAME:

☐ BACKGROUND CHECK

PHONE: (......)................ DRIVER'S LICENSE #:...................................... EXPIRATION: ...../...../...... LICENSE PLATE:..............................

VEHICLE YEAR, MAKE & MODEL:.. # OF PASSENGER SEATBELTS: ....

CAR INSURANCE COMPANY:... POLICY #:... EXPIRATION:...../...../......

DRIVING LOG:

DATE	EVENT/DESTINATION	DRIVER SIGNATURE	TROOP LEADER SIGNATURE

NAME:

☐ BACKGROUND CHECK

PHONE: (......)................ DRIVER'S LICENSE #:...................................... EXPIRATION: ...../...../...... LICENSE PLATE:..............................

VEHICLE YEAR, MAKE & MODEL:.. # OF PASSENGER SEATBELTS: ....

CAR INSURANCE COMPANY:... POLICY #:... EXPIRATION:...../...../......

DRIVING LOG:

DATE	EVENT/DESTINATION	DRIVER SIGNATURE	TROOP LEADER SIGNATURE

"When you're knocked down, get right back up and never listen to anyone who says you shouldn't go on."

FORMER SECRETARY OF STATE HILLARY CLINTON

NAME:

☐ BACKGROUND CHECK

PHONE: (......)................ DRIVER'S LICENSE #:.................................... EXPIRATION: ...../...../...... LICENSE PLATE:...............................

VEHICLE YEAR, MAKE & MODEL:... # OF PASSENGER SEATBELTS: ....

CAR INSURANCE COMPANY:.. POLICY #:.. EXPIRATION:...../...../......

DRIVING LOG:

DATE	EVENT/DESTINATION	DRIVER SIGNATURE	TROOP LEADER SIGNATURE

NAME:

☐ BACKGROUND CHECK

PHONE: (......)................ DRIVER'S LICENSE #:.................................... EXPIRATION: ...../...../...... LICENSE PLATE:...............................

VEHICLE YEAR, MAKE & MODEL:... # OF PASSENGER SEATBELTS: ....

CAR INSURANCE COMPANY:.. POLICY #:.. EXPIRATION:...../...../......

DRIVING LOG:

DATE	EVENT/DESTINATION	DRIVER SIGNATURE	TROOP LEADER SIGNATURE

VOLUNTEER DRIVER LOG

NAME:

☐ BACKGROUND CHECK

PHONE: (......).................. DRIVER'S LICENSE #:.................................... EXPIRATION: ...../...../...... LICENSE PLATE:..............................

VEHICLE YEAR, MAKE & MODEL:.. # OF PASSENGER SEATBELTS: ....

CAR INSURANCE COMPANY:.. POLICY #:... EXPIRATION:...../...../......

DRIVING LOG:

DATE	EVENT/DESTINATION	DRIVER SIGNATURE	TROOP LEADER SIGNATURE

NAME:

☐ BACKGROUND CHECK

PHONE: (......).................. DRIVER'S LICENSE #:.................................... EXPIRATION: ...../...../...... LICENSE PLATE:..............................

VEHICLE YEAR, MAKE & MODEL:.. # OF PASSENGER SEATBELTS: ....

CAR INSURANCE COMPANY:.. POLICY #:... EXPIRATION:...../...../......

DRIVING LOG:

DATE	EVENT/DESTINATION	DRIVER SIGNATURE	TROOP LEADER SIGNATURE

"If you don't know what you're here to do then just do some good."
POET & ACTIVIST MAYA ANGELOU

NAME:

☐ BACKGROUND CHECK

PHONE: (......)................. DRIVER'S LICENSE #:...................................... EXPIRATION: ...../...../...... LICENSE PLATE:...............................

VEHICLE YEAR, MAKE & MODEL:.. # OF PASSENGER SEATBELTS: ....

CAR INSURANCE COMPANY:.. POLICY #:... EXPIRATION:...../...../.....

DRIVING LOG:

DATE	EVENT/DESTINATION	DRIVER SIGNATURE	TROOP LEADER SIGNATURE

NAME:

☐ BACKGROUND CHECK

PHONE: (......)................. DRIVER'S LICENSE #:...................................... EXPIRATION: ...../...../...... LICENSE PLATE:...............................

VEHICLE YEAR, MAKE & MODEL:.. # OF PASSENGER SEATBELTS: ....

CAR INSURANCE COMPANY:.. POLICY #:... EXPIRATION:...../...../.....

DRIVING LOG:

DATE	EVENT/DESTINATION	DRIVER SIGNATURE	TROOP LEADER SIGNATURE

VOLUNTEER DRIVER LOG

NAME:

☐ BACKGROUND CHECK

PHONE: (......)................ DRIVER'S LICENSE #:.................................... EXPIRATION: ...../...../...... LICENSE PLATE:..............................

VEHICLE YEAR, MAKE & MODEL:.. # OF PASSENGER SEATBELTS: ....

CAR INSURANCE COMPANY:.. POLICY #:.. EXPIRATION:...../...../......

DRIVING LOG:

DATE	EVENT/DESTINATION	DRIVER SIGNATURE	TROOP LEADER SIGNATURE

NAME:

☐ BACKGROUND CHECK

PHONE: (......)................ DRIVER'S LICENSE #:.................................... EXPIRATION: ...../...../...... LICENSE PLATE:..............................

VEHICLE YEAR, MAKE & MODEL:.. # OF PASSENGER SEATBELTS: ....

CAR INSURANCE COMPANY:.. POLICY #:.. EXPIRATION:...../...../......

DRIVING LOG:

DATE	EVENT/DESTINATION	DRIVER SIGNATURE	TROOP LEADER SIGNATURE

Made in United States
Orlando, FL
05 May 2022

17581926R10083